# OR EVEN EAGLE FLEW

# OR EVEN EAGLE FLEW

## HARRY TURTLEDOVE

Prince
of
Cats

Literary
Productions

# CHAPTER ONE

THE TRAIN from Cleveland to Montreal chugged to a stop at the border between the USA and Canada. The woman near the front of the car picked up the *Plain Dealer* she'd bought before she got on. The war news from the Low Countries and France was just as lousy now as it had been when she first looked at it a few hours before. She frowned and put the paper back on the seat beside her.

She'd just fished *Gone with the Wind* out of her purse instead when two uniformed American customs men walked into the car from the one ahead of it. They paused in the aisle by her. "Let me see your papers, ma'am," one of them said.

"Oh, for Chrissake, Otis!" the other one exploded. "That there's a dame, case you didn't notice. *She* ain't gonna run off to England to fly planes for the stupid King."

"Never can tell," the first customs man—Otis—said. "She kinda looks like Charles Lindbergh, know what I mean?" He turned back to the woman. "Your papers."

Without a word, she handed him her passport. She'd heard the comparison with Lindbergh before, and didn't care for it (she happened to know he didn't, either). She liked his isolationist, America First politics even less.

Otis opened the passport to the page with her name and photo. "Putnam, Amelia E.," he read, and scribbled on a sheet in his clipboard. "Purpose of visiting Canada, Mrs. Putnam?"

"Visiting friends," she answered, looking up at him over the tops of her reading glasses. Except on a few formal documents like this, she didn't use her husband's —now her ex-husband's—last name. It came in handy here; her own would have caused problems.

"'Visiting friends.'" Otis wrote that down, too. He handed back the passport. "Enjoy your stay."

"Thank you."

As the customs men walked down the aisle, the other one said, "See? Told ya so."

"Ah, shut up," Otis told him.

They checked more passports, and lingered longest with two men in their twenties: one tall and carrot-topped, the other medium-sized, with a Clark Gable mustache.

The customs men gave the young Americans a much tougher time than they had the woman.

Amelia Earhart—the name she used almost all the

time—smiled to herself. If the smile seemed sour, then it did, that was all. Those young fellows weren't *dames*, after all. It was reasonable, even to a customs man, to think they might know something about flying.

They had to get their suitcases down from the overhead rack so the inspectors could paw through them. They passed muster, though; the customs men went on to inflict themselves on the next car back from the locomotive.

Pretty soon—not soon enough to suit A.E., but pretty soon—the train got rolling again. The redhead and the guy who wished he were Clark Gable both let out muffled whoops when they crossed into Canada. "They aren't as smart as they think they are!" said the guy with the red hair.

*They sure aren't,* A.E. thought. She picked up *Gone with the Wind* again. Scarlett was eating grits and dried peas with Aunt Pittypat, and swearing to herself she'd never touch them again once she had money. A.E. kept reading as the train rolled on to Montreal.

# CHAPTER TWO

WHEN THEY REACHED THE STATION, she grabbed her own small suitcase—she hadn't thought the customs men would search it, and they hadn't—and hurried to the cab rank. Quick as she was, those two young men were quicker. They piled into a taxi and roared away.

Well, there were more. "Where to, *Madame*?" asked the driver after she got into his Chevy.

"The Mount Royal Hotel, please." Something in the way the man looked and talked made her add, "Uh, *s'il vous plait.*"

He opened his eyes a little wider and smiled. *"Vous parlez français?"*

*"Je regrette, mais un petit peu."* A.E. had taken French in school, then forgotten most of it till she had to dust it off to try to talk with French officials in Africa on her round-the-world flight. She was glad to get in a little

practice here; where she planned to go, she'd need all she had and then some.

*"C'est meilleur que rien,"* the cab driver said. A.E. nodded. Even a little *was* better than nothing. The cabby put the car in gear and started for the hotel.

The Mount Royal wasn't far from the station. One thing stood out, though, even in that short distance: unlike the United States, Canada was a country at war. At least half the men on the street wore khaki, RCN navy blue, or the slightly brighter blue of the RCAF.

People here looked worried, too, in a way Americans didn't. In the USA, the European war was a noise in another room, nothing to get excited about. Canada was in it up to her eyebrows, and it wasn't going well. Short-pants kids on corners sold newspapers whose headlines, in English and in French, shouted about how badly it was going.

No more than fifteen minutes after the taxi left the station, it pulled up in front of the Mount Royal. "Sixty cents, ma'am," the driver said—in English, to make sure he wasn't misunderstood.

"Here." A.E. gave him a US dollar bill; she hadn't had the chance to change any money. He took it without a word. American and Canadian money were as near on a par with each other as made no difference. When he started to make change, she told him, "Don't bother."

*"Merci beaucoup!"* he exclaimed, pleased back into his first language. He hopped out of the car, hustled around to open her door for her, and hauled her suitcase

out of the trunk. A bellhop took it from him before A.E. could.

She checked in, got her key, and rode the elevator to the third floor. The key, which had 327 stamped into it, worked in the lock of the room whose door had that number on it. The bellboy set the suitcase on the bed. She gave him a quarter: US again.

It fazed him no more than the greenback had bothered the taxi man. He touched a couple of fingers to the edge of his pillbox cap in an almost military salute. "Thank you, ma'am," he said. "You need anything here, ask for Lyon Sprague. That's me." He tapped his chest.

"I will. Thanks," she said. Lyon Sprague decamped. A couple of minutes later, so did A.E. She'd half-hoped someone would have been waiting for her in the lobby. No such luck though. Instead of summoning the elevator, she walked down the stairs.

Somehow, she wasn't all that surprised when she discovered the redheaded young man and his friend with the mustache there ahead of her. "No messages for either one of us?" the tall redhead was asking the desk clerk. "No letters? Not for either one of us?"

"I am very sorry, *Monsieur*." The hotel man spread his hands in a good facsimile of regret. "I cannot give you what I do not have."

"Nothing from Colonel Sweeny?" the guy with the mustache persisted. A.E. nodded to herself. Yes, they'd all shown up at the Mount Royal Hotel for the same reason.

But the desk clerk shook his head. "Nothing from anyone," he said firmly. He did unbend enough to point towards a very small man sitting on a sofa looking at a magazine about flying planes. "You might inquire of him. He has been asking after messages, too." By the way a muscle in his cheek twitched, the little guy had been less polite than these two.

The redhead and the man with the mustache went over to the short fellow. A.E. drifted that way, too. When the man on the sofa stood up, she saw he wasn't even five feet tall.

"Desk clerk says we're all in the same boat," the redhead said.

"Yeah—the *Titanic*," the short guy said with a sour laugh. He stuck out his hand. "I'm Vern Keough. Shorty, they call me—can't imagine why. I'm a pilot and a parachute jumper out of New York. I used to be five nine till I landed on my head a couple of times."

"Gene Tobin—Red, if you want," the tall man said, shaking with the short one. His buddy was Andy Mamedoff. They were both pilots from Los Angeles.

A.E. came up to them. "I think I may be in that boat with you, too," she said.

They looked her over. She'd seen that look too many times before. *You can't be. You're a woman,* it said. But then Mamedoff's eyes widened. She'd seen that happen before, too. He had a few years on the other two, so he might have paid more attention when she was in the news a lot. "You're—" he said, and didn't go on.

She nodded. "That's right. I'm Amelia Earhart. I aim to fly for the *Armée de l'Air*, too."

"But you're a woman." Red Tobin pointed out the obvious.

"I'm a pilot. I'm a darn good pilot," she replied. "France is in deep enough, I bet they won't care that I can't pee standing up. And the Nazis are horrible enough, they need stopping from whoever can stop them."

"Well, you sure aren't wrong about that," Mamedoff said. "And if they do let you fly, the publicity will bring more flyers from the States."

A.E. nodded. "The same thing crossed my mind."

Shorty Keough said, "Now Colonel Sweeny better come through. Not like I've got cash burning a hole in my pocket." Tobin and Mamedoff nodded at that. They wouldn't be rich; they were just getting started in life. A.E. had a good deal more money with her than all three of them put together, odds were.

Red chuckled without much humor. "When I started talking with Sweeny's people back in L.A., they wanted me to fly for Finland against the Russians. But Finland went belly-up, so now it's France against the Nazis." He shrugged. "They're all so-and-sos." A.E. judged he would have said something stronger had she been another man.

She nodded again anyhow. "They are. I don't have much use for war and killing, but people like Stalin and Hitler won't stop till somebody stops them."

"There you go!" Andy Mamedoff made as if to clap his hands.

"We aren't gonna be the ones who stop them unless Sweeny's stuff shows up," Tobin said. "I came this far on promises, but it's not like we can get across the Atlantic on them."

Once more, A.E.'s head bobbed up and down. Thanks to the USA's neutrality rules, going to fight in Europe's latest war could cost Americans their citizenship. A.E. thought she could make a living anywhere in the world, but she had experience and a reputation these young men couldn't hope to match.

"If Sweeny's stuff doesn't show up ..." Vern Keough made a fist. It wasn't a very big fist, but it summed up what A.E. was thinking, too.

A.E. WENT to the bar with the three young American men. They had a drink, then another one. While they drank, they called down curses on Charles Sweeny's head. A.E. didn't swear as foully or regularly as her new-met comrades-in-arms, but she had a knack for being funny and insulting without cussing. They seemed to appreciate it.

"Didn't know what you were like for real," Red Tobin said. "You're okay, though. Better'n okay." The other two men from the States nodded.

"Thanks," she said. Acceptance warmed her more than the rye did.

The bellhop called Lyon Sprague came up to them. He carried a tray with four envelopes on it. "You are the *Messieurs* Tobin, Putnam, Mamedoff, and Keough?" he said.

"I'm not a *Monsieur*, but I'm Putnam," A.E. said. To the Yanks, she added, "Married name." The bellboy gave her a dubious look, but two dollars cured it. She got her envelope with the others.

The envelope held a ticket on the night train to Halifax, Nova Scotia, and a scribbled note. *Stay in the station after other people leave. Talk about flying so our man will know you. Be loud.*

Everyone had a ticket to Halifax and the same note in almost the same words. "Well, hell," Andy Mamedoff said. "If I'd known we weren't gonna spend the night, I wouldn't've checked in." He made wings of his hands and mimed money flying away.

"So it goes," Red Tobin agreed. "And it has went. Only good news is, this joint ain't fancy enough to cost a whole lot."

They took two cabs back to the train station. They might all have fit into one, but their luggage wouldn't. A.E. rode with Tobin. "How much flying time do you have?" she asked.

He laughed sheepishly. "Less than my logbook says I do, but enough to know what I'm doing. Like Shorty said back at the bar, I'll fly in any air force except Hitler's or Stalin's."

"That sounds good," A.E. said. It also sounded like a recipe for getting yourself killed, something she didn't mention. Nobody became a fighter pilot in the hope of living a long, quiet life.

Most of the people on the train to Halifax were Canadian soldiers in khaki. When they found out A.E. and her friends were American, they asked the same question over and over again: "Why isn't the United States in the war?"

"Don't blame us," A.E. and the men said, over and over and over again. She didn't think it did much good.

When the train pulled into Halifax, the soldiers and the Canadian civilians had places to go. The four Americans hung around on the platform. As instructed, they chattered loudly about planes and flying.

After an hour or so, a short, squat man in a trench coat who'd jammed the brim of his fedora down low over his eyes walked up to them. A cigarette dangled from the corner of his mouth. He couldn't have looked more like a movie spy if he'd come straight from central casting.

"You are the Americans?" he asked in a heavy French accent.

"Not us. We're a church group from Melbourne, Australia," Red said.

A.E. kicked him in the ankle. "We're the Americans," she said quickly. "Don't worry about him. He likes to make jokes."

The man in the trench coat shrugged. "It matters not. If he shoots down the *Boches*—if you all shoot down the *Boches*—that matters. Come with me, *s'il vous plaît*."

He led them through back rooms at the station and through dripping alleys. He acted like a movie spy trying to shake off a tail. At last, in a bare room lit by a dim bulb, he opened a safe and handed each of them a manila envelope. "Travel documents and money," he said.

After A.E. opened the envelope's metal clasp, she found it held 2,500 francs and a safe-conduct from the French consul-general in Montreal with her photo and physical characteristics. It stated she was of "indeterminate" nationality but should be permitted to enter France.

Shorty Keough held up his new bankroll. "How much is this in dollars?"

"About fifty," the guy with the fedora answered unwillingly. "Now you should go to the harbor. The *Guingamp* sails at seven."

A.E. eyed her watch. It was already past three. By the time they got to the harbor, dawn was breaking. The *Guingamp* was a rustbucket freighter, part of a convoy bound for France. A.E. recognized the stench floating out of her hold. "I'll be darned if she's not hauling mules," she said.

"Whole lot of mules," Red Tobin agreed.

None of the sailors spoke English. The skipper did, a little. He had room for only two of them. Mamedoff and

Keough stayed. A.E. left with Tobin. They found spaces on another, equally grimy, freighter, the *Pierre L.D.* A.E. got a cabin all to herself. It was just about big enough to turn around in, as long as you were careful. Red bunked in the same kind of cabin, only he shared it with three other guys.

As soon as the convoy left the harbor and started zigzagging across the Atlantic, A.E. discovered a new reason to prefer flying. She had a strong stomach; she'd been airsick only a handful of times. The Atlantic's roll and pitch, though, proved too much for her. She did not enjoy the first couple of days at sea very much.

After that, the ocean got milder or she got used to it. She could visit the galley without rushing to the head or the rail as soon as she finished eating. They had a phonograph. Red played American records. The platters the French sailors spun were all about the war.

"You can tell why they fight, that's for sure," Tobin said, and he didn't speak a word of French.

A.E. nodded. "You can," she agreed. "If only they were doing better." The little news they got at sea came from the shortwave radio. Her French was improving with practice, but still wasn't good. Neither was any of the news.

# CHAPTER THREE

GERMAN U-BOATS WERE on everyone's mind. A British destroyer escorting the convoy depth-charged what it thought was one. Every sailor on the *Pierre L.D.* stayed at action stations for hours afterwards. No torpedoes tore into the freighters, though. Two weeks after leaving Halifax, the convoy steamed into St. Nazaire. A.E. and Red met up with Shorty and Mamedoff on the pier. The other Americans' travel had been every bit as delightful as theirs.

They'd hardly got off the docks before they realized everything in France had gone to hell while they crawled across the Atlantic. This wasn't just a country fighting a war—it was a country losing a war, and losing badly. No one in St. Nazaire had time for four Americans washed up on the lee shore of disaster.

At last, they found a harried official who grudged them half an hour he clearly resented. "I can give you train tickets to Paris, but the train does not depart until Monday," he said. "Until then, I can put you up here." He sighed. "I suppose I can put you up here."

Only they didn't leave Monday. The French bureaucrats gave them three more days of grief. "Why should we help you?" the last one said. "According to your documents, your nationality is indeterminate. What are you?"

"We're Americans. You know damn well we're Americans," Red Tobin snapped. His patience had worn very thin. So had A.E.'s.

"You have no passports," the Frenchman said.

"Our government won't let us travel to a war zone on 'em," Shorty Keough said.

"I do. They didn't worry about me." A.E. produced hers.

The functionary gave it a fishy stare. "What are you doing with these men, *Madame* Poot-nahm?" What his accent did to her married name was a caution. "Are you their mother?"

"I'm a pilot, same as they are," she answered, as evenly as she could. "Putnam is my ex-husband's last name. Mine is Earhart."

He needed a couple of seconds before that sank in. *"Nom d'un nom!"* he muttered, and then, "You are the famous Amelia Earhart?"

"That's me." A.E. didn't like to trade on her fame, but it came in handy every so often. "So how about you let us have those tickets for Paris we're supposed to get?"

She didn't know whether the ploy would work, but

they were on the next train to the French capital. "Gotta hand it to you, ma'am," Andy Mamedoff said as they squeezed into a crowded car. "That was terrific."

"Thanks," A.E. said. "And for God's sake call me Amelia. Otherwise I'll think we've got that damned French pencil pusher along with us."

He grinned at her. "You're okay, you know that?"

"Well, I try," she said, just as the train began to move.

FROM ST. NAZAIRE to Paris was about two hundred miles. The train seemed to stop every half hour or so. One of the stops, at Le Mans, was very bad. A westbound train had also stopped, on the track next to theirs. Half the cars had been shot up from the air. They were pocked with bullet and shell holes; only a few windows still had glass in them. And half the French soldiers in the cars looked to have been shot up, too. They were bloody; they were bandaged; their faces were pale and full of pain. A fellow with a Red Cross armband tenderly helped a wounded man smoke a cigarette.

"Nazi bastards," Mamedoff ground out.

"If we spotted a German troop train, or a column of trucks ..." Red Tobin said slowly. "It's war. This is what we signed up for."

A.E. had thought about shooting down enemy pilots in 109s or 110s or bombers. She hadn't thought about shooting up luckless foot soldiers who might not even be able to shoot back. But Red was right. That also came with the job.

After a mournful toot from the whistle, the train rolled on toward Paris.

THE HOTEL in the City of Light was, not to put too fine a point on it, a fleabag. Tobin, Keough, and Mamedoff shared a room. It had one narrow bed. How they decided who got to use it, A.E. didn't know. She had a room to herself. It was bigger than her cabin on the *Pierre L.D.*, but not much. An almost equally tiny bathroom lurked down at the end of the hall.

No one slept the night after they got in. German planes bombed Paris. What sounded like every antiaircraft gun in the world tried to shoot them down. A bomb hit no more than 150 yards from the hotel. The noise was like the end of the world. The building jumped as if someone had kicked it in the behind. A.E.'s window rattled, but didn't blow in.

Next morning, over croissants and strong coffee at a café around the corner, Red managed a crooked grin. "Boy, that was fun," he said.

*"Merde!"* Andy Mamedoff had started picking up French.

That word, and others like it, came in handy when the Americans tried to get any *Armée de l'Air* officials to pay attention to them. They didn't have much luck. In a way, A.E. understood it. The Germans were surging forward everywhere. Paris itself looked like falling soon. The British and French troops who hadn't made it across the Channel to England had surrendered to the Nazis. In the face of catastrophe, who could get excited about a few possible pilots? All the same ...

"Least they can do is give us a medical exam and put us in planes," Shorty Keough groused. "How can we do worse than they're doing already?"

"They haven't got time for us," A.E. said. "We're uninvited guests in a house where someone's dying."

"Where everybody's dying," Red Tobin amended, and she didn't try to tell him he was wrong.

She did say, "Something I've seen in French planes, you guys need to remember. You pull the throttle out for more power and push it in for less, right?"

"Sure," Andy Mamedoff said. Shorty and Red nodded.

"Sure if it's an American plane or an English one or even one from Germany," A.E. said. "France and Italy do it backwards. With their planes, you push the throttle in for more juice and pull it out to ease back. You can kill yourself if you forget. I almost did once."

"Thanks," Red said. "That's worth knowing, all right."

"If we ever get into a French plane it will be, anyhow," Shorty said.

"This country is going down the drain," Mamedoff

said, and nobody tried to contradict him, either. He went on, "I came over here to fight the goddamn Nazis, not to surrender to them."

"None of us has proper papers. Except Amelia, I mean," Red said.

Mamedoff exhaled through his nose. "Papers are the least of my worries if the Germans catch us." He was Jewish. He didn't make a big deal out of it, but the *Gestapo* wouldn't care about that.

A couple of days later, they finally did get called in for medicals. The doc who examined A.E. was short and dumpy and bald with a fringe of gray. He spoke some English. Along with her bits of French, they managed to understand each other. Before long, she wasn't sure she wanted to. "You are something out of the ordinary," he remarked.

"I'm a pilot. I'm a good pilot. If I ever get the chance, I can help France," she said.

"France?" He waved that aside. "France, *c'est morte.*" *France is dead.* It wasn't a thought A.E. hadn't had herself, but she hated hearing it from a Frenchman. She also hated the way the guy's hands wandered. It wasn't the first time that kind of thing had happened, but it was the first time in quite a while.

"Watch yourself, Charlie," she snapped.

"If you are friendly, I promise you will pass the medical," he said.

"Friendly, huh? I'm going to pass the medical or I'm gonna beat the living crap out of you. Your choice. How about that?" At five eight, she was at least three inches taller than he was. She was also in much better shape. She figured she could do exactly what she threatened.

By the way he licked his lips, by the way his eyes widened behind his steel-framed spectacles, so did he. "You don't have to be so, so *masculine* about it," he said.

"Just make sure my papers look the way they're supposed to. I know enough *français* to catch you if you try to pull a fast one, too." A.E. hoped she was right. That *masculine* made her want to laugh more than it made her mad. It wasn't the first time she'd got called a dyke. Nowhere close. Way too much of the world thought any woman who tried to get ahead in a man's profession had to be butch.

Despite passing their medicals, the Americans kept not getting sent anywhere that had airplanes. Andy and Shorty and Red went out and got magnificently smashed; their piteous state the next morning showed what a big one they'd tied on. Some of the things they stifled, not quite soon enough, when they noticed A.E. was in earshot made her sure they'd done some serious screwing to go with their serious drinking. That didn't embarrass her—it amused her. Boys would be boys.

They'd surely long since run through the 2,500 francs they'd got in Halifax. One way or another, they kept themselves in funds without putting the bite on her. She liked them better for that.

# CHAPTER FOUR

ON THE TENTH OF JUNE, A.E. woke to see the sun rise red through man-made, foul-smelling fog. The French were sending up smokescreens and burning crude oil to shield Paris from German bombers. She'd understood for a while that the City of Light would fall soon. Realizing the French understood it, too, was like a punch in the gut.

Over the usual meager breakfast—what was *wrong* with bacon and eggs or something like that, for crying out loud?—Andy Mamedoff said, "We've gotta get out of here while we still can."

"How do you aim to pay the hotel bill?" Shorty asked, so maybe the men weren't keeping themselves in funds after all.

"I don't," Mamedoff said calmly. "I aim to skip."

A.E. could have paid their bill along with hers. Instead, she skipped with them. It distressed her much less than she'd imagined it could. Everything was breaking down. With the Nazis bound to march into Paris soon, the people who ran the hotel had more to worry about than foreigners who didn't pay what they owed.

The *Gar de l'Est* was chaos compounded. Everyone was trying to make it aboard a train heading away from the oncoming Germans. The Americans literally fought their way onto one bound for Tours in the southwest. What was left of the French government was on its way there, too. There was an airstrip not far from town. Maybe the fight could go on after the swastika flew over Paris. Maybe.

It was standing room only in the car. A lot of the standees were soldiers. A *poilu* breathed garlic and sour wine into A.E.'s face as he said, "I don't want to give in. My leaders are spineless *cochons*, but not me."

"Good," she answered.

They reached Tours early in the afternoon, just in time to dive into a ditch as the *Luftwaffe* bombed the town. Then they tried to get a car to take them to the air base. They had no luck, and hoofed it instead. A.E. wore comfortable shoes, but what was comfortable in town wasn't so much for what turned out to be a five-mile hike. She wasn't the only one with barking dogs by the time they got there, either.

At least the *Armée de l'Air* officers at the base seemed to know who they were and why they'd come to France. One of them pointed to a two-seat Potez 63 heavy fighter or light bomber at the edge of a dirt runway. "We will train you up on this *avion*," he said in a mixture of English and French.

"For God's sake remember the backwards throttle," A.E. warned her comrades. "You really will kill yourselves if you don't."

"Gotcha," Red said, and sketched a salute.

"Our own side is liable to shoot us down if we go up in one of those. It looks a lot like a Messerschmitt 110," Andy Mamedoff added.

The same thing had occurred to A.E. "Maybe the Nazis won't shoot at us so much," she said.

"Here's hoping," Shorty agreed.

THEY DID NOT GET TRAINED on that Potez 63. Less than half an hour after the French officer pointed it out to them, a Stuka screamed down out of the sky and strafed it, leaving it a burning wreck. Another French fighter, this one actually airworthy, downed the German dive bomber as it tried to climb away. It smashed to earth only a couple of hundred yards from the plane it had killed.

Quietly, A.E. said, "You hope the crash killed them before the fire started." The other three Americans all nodded. Like her, they'd seen mishaps before. Only this was no mishap. The French pilot had meant to do just what he did. If they went up there in fighter planes,

German pilots would try their damnedest to do that to them. The thought was sobering.

They ate well that night, washing down roast pork with pretty good red wine. The French seemed to believe A.E. could fly fighters. They ran up a tent for her by the ones the men slept in, and gave her a cot with a skinny mattress and a rough wool blanket. She slept like a rock.

News came from the north, by radio and by fleeing soldiers and civilians. Paris was declared an open city to keep the Germans from bombing it flat. The *Wehrmacht* wouldn't just march in; it would parade in. The Americans wouldn't have much chance to fly in France after all. Surrender couldn't be more than days away.

WORD THAT FRANCE had asked Germany for an armistice came over the radio on June 17. "Well, now it's official," Red Tobin said glumly. "We aren't gonna be aces in the *Armée de l'Air*."

"What *will* the Nazis do with us if they catch us?" Andy wondered. "Not like we've got passports or anything." A.E. did, of course, but felt oddly happier because he didn't remind her of it.

Shorty sliced a thumb across his throat. "What do the Nazis do *to* us, is what you mean."

"Maybe we can get to Bordeaux. Maybe we can squeeze onto a ship bound for England from there," Red said. "If I can't fight the *Luftwaffe* in the *Armée de l'Air*, I'll do it in the RAF."

"What do you think our chances are?" Shorty asked. Tobin didn't answer. Anyone could see the odds weren't good.

"I have another idea." A.E. spoke for the first time. The three men all looked at her. They did her the courtesy of taking her seriously. She'd earned that by not trading on her fame with them and by not looking for any special treatment because she was a woman. She went on, "There are a couple of more of those Potez two-seaters out past the woods." She gestured. "If we get into them, we're only two hours from England—as long as we remember which way the throttle goes, anyhow."

"They'll be guarded," Mamedoff said gloomily. "How do you aim to get past the sentries?"

"The government isn't here any more. The Germans were getting too close. They've all gone to Bordeaux themselves. We can say we've been ordered to take the planes there," A.E. said. "The soldiers will believe us. They'll think the big shots will want to run away to England themselves."

"Maybe. Or maybe not," Andy said. "Suppose they ask to see our orders. What happens then?"

"Leave that to me." A.E. sounded more confident than she felt. She knew the kind chance she'd be taking. Even next to the risk of getting shot down in flames, the danger wasn't small. But she saw no safe way out of a country about to surrender to its worst enemy.

# CHAPTER FIVE

THEY TIPTOED through the forest in pre-sunrise murk the next morning. A.E. wondered whether they should have headed for Bordeaux after all. They *might* still have found a ship. Then they were out of the trees and on damp grass again, the Potez 63s only fifty yards ahead.

"Halt! Who goes there?" a sentry barked. He held a rifle. Even before sunrise, the bayonet fixed to the end of the barrel glinted nastily.

"We are the American flyers. The American flyers who came to fly for the Republic." A.E. was the only one with enough French to talk to him. She went through her spiel; she'd lost sleep rehearsing it in her head more times than she could count.

*"Vive la République!"* Andy Mamedoff added, as if on cue. That was a fair chunk of the French he'd learned. Of the clean French, anyway.

"Advance and be recognized," the sentry said. A.E. waved her comrades up with her in case they didn't follow. The sentry's two chums also showed themselves. That relieved her; there'd been three soldiers here when she'd checked the day before. The fellow who was doing the talking went on, "Show me your orders, if you please."

This was the tricky part. She took a deep breath before answering. "*Mais certainement.* I have a copy for each of you." She handed each soldier a sheet of paper folded in thirds horizontally. Inside each folded sheet was a hundred-dollar bill.

The fellow who'd questioned her had bushy eyebrows. They jumped when he saw the American money. One of the other soldiers exclaimed softly. The Frenchmen put their heads together for a moment. When they drew apart, the one who did the talking waved the Americans forward with an oddly courtly gesture, like a headwaiter offering a fine table. "Carry out your orders, friends of the Republic!" he said.

Trying not to show how weak her knees had got, A.E. walked up the two Potez 63s. The other Americans followed. The French planes reminded her not only of Messerschmitt 110s but also of the Lockheed Electra 10 in which she'd flown around the world. They were a bit smaller and slimmer—they were built for combat, not to carry passengers—but had similar lines and those twin tailfins.

She and Andy, the medium-sized people, got into

one plane. Red and Vernon Keough, the long and short of it, climbed into the other. "Remember, the throttle works backwards," she said one more time before they closed the canopies. "Follow me if you can."

"Yes, ma'am," Red said, and gave her a wave that was half a salute. "See you in England."

She strapped herself into the pilot's seat. Mamedoff took the one behind it, which faced the other way and let him use the machine gun that defended the Potez against attacks from the rear. She hoped—she prayed, though not much given to praying—he wouldn't have to.

At least he hadn't tried to claim the pilot's seat himself. She had more experience than he did, and the bit of French she knew let her make some sense of the instrument panel. Not all men would have cared about any of that, but he owned sense enough to know it mattered.

The spade grip on the end of the stick had a red button on it. That was for the plane's forward-facing guns. Again, she hoped she wouldn't need it. She'd done a lot of flying, but not in combat, not yet.

She checked the fuel gauge. If the Potez was dry, she had a whole new problem, and not enough C-notes to spread around to solve it. But the gauge showed the tanks were better than half full. Was that enough to fly 350-odd miles?

A.E. laughed mirthlessly. She'd find out. So would Shorty and Red. How much gas did their plane carry?

Where were the engine starters? She found them, or

hoped she did. When she hit the one labeled G, the left engine roared to life. The one marked D fired up the engine and prop on the right. A moment later, the other Potez's props began to spin. Red gave her a thumbs-up from its cockpit.

Gently, as if walking on eggs, she pushed the throttle in a little. That felt unnatural, but the plane began to roll. She hadn't been so careful or so nervous since her first takeoff. She steered the Potez's nose into the wind, not that there was much, and gave it more gas.

It bumped over the dirt and grass of the field. She was more used to that kind of takeoff than to the smooth sort that came on paved runways. Everything she did was by eye and by feel. When she pulled back on the stick, the Potez's nose went up. As soon as she knew it would stay airborne, she let out an Indian war whoop.

From the rear-facing seat, Andy Mamedoff bawled, "Red got off the ground, too!"

When A.E. understood him, she whooped again. After gaining some altitude, she cranked the wheels up into their wells. There was probably a hydraulic system to do it the easy way, but she couldn't find the control on the instrument panel. She didn't care. This worked.

She flew north at what the airspeed indicator said was three hundred kilometers an hour. That was two hundred miles an hour, or a little less. The Potez was faster than her old Electra, but not a whole lot. Against a Messerschmitt or a Hurricane, it would be in deep.

She had a compass. She could see shadows on the

ground. England was a big target. She figured she'd find it. Nothing to worry about on that score, not the way there had been when she and Fred Noonan found Howland Island, a tiny speck of sand sticking up a few feet out of the endless, endless miles of the Pacific. Even drunk, as he often was, Fred had by God known how to navigate.

The altimeter, of course, read in meters. A meter was a yard, close enough. She stayed between three hundred and six hundred meters—one to two thousand feet. That way, she didn't have to worry about oxygen. And if she wasn't up very high, fewer people on the ground would spot her. That could matter. By now, she had to be crossing territory the Germans had overrun.

This plane had a rearview mirror at the top of the windscreen. She'd never seen that in any civilian model. When you flew into combat, though, you needed to see what was coming up behind you before it shot you down. At the moment, the only thing behind her was Red's Potez. They both buzzed along as serenely as if no one had ever heard of war.

But people had. There clogging a highway was a German column: tanks, halftracks, trucks, motorcycles, guns, horse-drawn wagons, countless foot soldiers in field gray. A.E.'s thumb slid toward the red button. If she put her nose down and shot them up ... She knew it was a bad idea, but it tempted her just the same.

Some of the infantrymen waved up at her. Sure as hell, they thought her Potez and Red's were Messerschmitt 110s. Instead of opening fire on them, she waggled her wings. If they thought her a friend, she needed to act like one.

She flew on. France was greener and more finely divided into fields than most parts of the United States. She eyed the fuel gauge. It had sunk under the halfway line, but she'd been going for more than an hour. She nodded to herself. She ought to have enough to get to England.

Did Red? He was still a few hundred yards behind her. He could make his own fuel calculations ... couldn't he? A.E. shrugged and kept going. If he ran out of gas, she couldn't do anything about it.

After a while, she reached the Channel. She remembered the fuss people had made the first time an airplane crossed it. That was in 1909; she couldn't recall whether Blériot's flight came before or after her twelfth birthday. Now it was just a ten-minute hop, with England on the far side.

England ... and the RAF. If a patrolling Hurricane or Spitfire spotted her plane, would the pilot take the Potez 63 for a Messerschmitt? Landing as soon as she could suddenly seemed like a real good idea. She cranked down the landing gear, hoping Red would notice.

The cold, choppy gray water down below gave way to land. A.E. saw no sign of the white cliffs of Dover—she had to be farther west. Well, that was all right. Everything down below looked green and lush, as it had on the other side of the Channel.

*Find a meadow big enough to land in,* she told herself. As soon as she did, she began circling and descending. She saw Red Tobin doing the same thing. She also saw, with some relief, that his plane's wheels were down, too.

Here came the ground. It wouldn't be as smooth as it looked. It never was. The plane touched, bounced, touched again. She slowed to a stop, remembering one more time to pull the throttle out instead of pushing it in. When they were just about stopped, she killed the engines, first the left, then the right. The props slowed to immobility. Silence seemed strange after the droning roar that had filled her since dawn.

"Good job, boss," Andy Mamedoff said. "You can pilot me any old time."

"Any landing you can walk away from is a good one," A.E. said. Red Tobin brought his Potez down. He landed rougher than she had, but he didn't do a noseover or a ground loop. After he shut down his engines, he waved to her. So did Shorty from the rear seat. She waved back.

When she opened the canopy, the air was fresh and cool, noticeably cooler than it had been down in Tours. And a farmer was stumping across a meadow toward the planes. He carried only a pitchfork, but he carried it with as much determination as if it were a Tommy gun.

"Don't try to get away!" he shouted. "I've called the soldiers, I have!"

"Good." A.E. unstrapped and climbed out of the cockpit. "They can take us to London. We're friends."

Her voice and her looks stopped the farmer in his tracks. "You're—you're ... her," he said. "I seen you in the newsreels, I did. Never thought you'd come down on my back pasture."

Three cars pulled up to the edge of the meadow. Helmeted men with rifles spilled out of them and trotted across the grass. A.E. ran a hand through her short, red-gold curls. The gesture was calculated to make them notice her, and it did. Like the farmer, a couple of them recognized her, too. She could watch word of who she was spread through the Englishmen.

Still, one of the soldiers began to raise his rifle. An older man with three chevrons on his sleeve—upside-down chevrons, to A.E.'s way of thinking—knocked the muzzle to one side. "Them ain't Germans," he said, and then, to the Americans, "Just who are you, and what are you doing here?"

Backed by Andy Mamedoff, A.E. began to explain. Red and Shorty walked over from their Potez and chimed in now and then. The longer the soldiers listened, the bigger their eyes got.

# CHAPTER SIX

LONDON. A.E. had thought her troubles, and the other Americans', would be over when they got to London. Instead, she found them just beginning. Colonel Charles Sweeny was not in town. Apparently, he'd been in France, though she'd never heard from him while she and the others were there. His nephew—who, just to confuse things, was named Charles Sweeny, too—was, but he carried less clout with the British than the more senior man did.

She and her friends made headlines. Typical was the one that said AMELIA, 3 OTHER YANKS FLY OUT OF FRANCE ONE JUMP AHEAD OF THE NAZIS. The younger Sweeny was delighted: that kind of publicity would draw more Americans across the Atlantic to fly for England. For the same reason, the US embassy was furious. By the way Ambassador Kennedy talked, he expected the swastika to fly from Buckingham Palace any day now, the way it was already flying from the Eiffel Tower.

The RAF ... The RAF blew hot and cold. At first, they wanted nothing to do with any of the four newly arrived Americans. Then they decided to let Red and Shorty and Andy train up to fly fighters ... but not A.E.

She had an unpleasant interview with Air Vice Marshal Trafford Leigh-Mallory, who seemed to have the power to bind and to loose. "Why won't you let me fly for you?" she demanded, blunt as usual. "I've got more flying time than my three friends put together."

Leigh-Mallory was a plump little man; he looked more like a clerk than a warrior. "The answer should be obvious," he replied. "You're a woman."

"So what?" she said. "Do you think the airplane will care?"

He steepled his fingertips. "Have you any experience whatever in fighter planes?"

"About thirty hours in the Curtiss Hawk," she replied. "Someone I know in the US Army let me try it out last year."

Leigh-Mallory made a sour face. He hadn't got the answer he wanted. "The Hawk's not up to snuff over here, you know. We have women ferrying aircraft from base to base. You may do that, if you like."

"You're wasting people that way. How many flyers have you got to spare?" she said. When he didn't come back right away, she knew she'd struck a nerve. She went on, "How much bad press in the States will you get if you don't let me try now?"

He turned a dull red. "That's blackmail."

"Not a bit," she said, thinking *It sure is*. "Let me try, doggone it. Send me to the same training school where you sent Red and Shorty and Andy. If I wash out, I wash out. But I bet I don't."

Could Leigh-Mallory have shot down planes with his glare, not a German fighter would have stayed airborne within five miles of him. "All right. All *right!*" he growled. "You're on my back, the bloody politicians are on my back, everyone's on my back. If you're so keen on getting yourself killed, I'll *send* you to Croydon. See how much you like it when your kite's on fire and you can't open the canopy to get out."

"This is what I came for," A.E. said, and wondered if she meant it.

THE OPERATIONAL TRAINING Unit at Croydon was about ten miles south of downtown London. Everything in England felt next door to everything else when you were used to the USA's wide open spaces. The barracks at the OTU were packed tight with apprentice pilots from England, Canada, South Africa, Poland, Czechoslovakia, France, and the three men from the USA.

As the French had at the base near Tours, the RAF rigged her a tent outside the building. With summer arriving, it wasn't too bad. Even if it had been, A.E. would have gone to hell before she complained.

She found out from Red Tobin what Air Vice Marshal Leigh-Mallory had meant when he snarled about politicians. "Yeah," Red said. "Somebody told me to talk to a guy named Robbie Robertson. He's an MP— you know, a member of Parliament—and he kind of specializes in getting foreigners into the RAF. So I talked to him, and I guess he pulled whatever strings he could pull, 'cause here we are."

"Here we are," she agreed.

They trained on Miles Masters. The two-seaters looked like undersized Hurricanes. Shorty Keough had to use a cushion under his behind and another at his back so he could see out and use the foot controls, but he managed. So did A.E.

"You have a notion what you're doing in the air, all right, ma'am," said the instructor who'd got into the raised rear seat, a sergeant old enough to have flown Sopwith Camels in the last war. "Almost embarrassed me to go up with you."

"I can fly," she said. "Shooting, though, and using that funny deflection sight ..." The Master had one machine gun in the right wing, to give trainees a taste of aerial shooting. Real fighters usually carried eight.

"Formation flying, too, I expect," the RAF veteran said. "Most civilian pilots haven't done much of that, or used the wireless the way we do here. That's why you came—that and so you could get into a Spitfire."

"That's why I came," A.E. echoed. Even the trainer's single machine gun reminded her this wasn't a game. Past shooting a few rats in the barn with her sister's .22, she'd had nothing to do with guns. And the rats in the barn couldn't shoot back. The rats in the *Luftwaffe*, on the other hand ...

"Won't be long," the sergeant pilot said. "We aim to get people into Spits quick as we can."

"I know," A.E. said. If the man's offhand comment wasn't a type specimen of British understatement, she didn't know what would be. German fighters and bombers were pounding southern England harder by the day. With Churchill bellowing defiance at the Nazis over the radio, Hitler knew he'd have to invade England to get her out of the war. He'd never do that if he didn't flatten the RAF first.

A.E. got her first chance in a Spitfire a few days later. The Miles Master, though pleasant to fly, was stolid like the family sedan. The Spitfire put her in mind of a sports car even before she climbed into the cockpit. It had the most perfect lines she'd ever seen on any airplane.

A smile stretched itself across her face. It got there before she realized it was even on the way. "When they look right, they fly right," she said to the RAF sergeant.

He beamed and nodded. "That's what they say, and for once they know what they're talking about."

The cockpit was cramped. It smelled of gasoline and oil and leather and sweat. The Spitfire wasn't new. New planes went to the pilots who were using them against the Nazis. New pilots learned on old, beat-up machines. A.E. strapped herself in and started the engine. Time to learn.

When the big Merlin thundered to life, that delighted smile made her face shine again. This was *power*! A Spitfire weighed little more than a Master, but its engine had to have close to twice the horsepower. She'd known that before, but, as with a lot of things, there was a lot of difference between knowing and experiencing.

Flying the Spit was like driving a Jaguar, too, after years of sedately tooling around in Plymouths and Fords. Except for her brief stretch in the Curtiss Hawk, she'd never flown a plane that could break three hundred miles per hour. Even the Hawk had to huff and puff to do it. The Spitfire managed without breathing hard.

And, despise him as she would, she soon saw why Air Vice Marshall Leigh-Mallory looked down his nose at the American fighter. The Spit outclassed it in speed, in climb, in maneuverability, and in high-altitude performance. She had to brace her elbow against the side of the cockpit to work the Spitfire's ailerons. Past that, it had no vices she could see.

She must have still had that silly smile on her face when she landed the Spit after forty-five exhilarating minutes, because the RAF instructor said, "Like it a bit, do you?"

"It's terrific!" A.E. exclaimed. "Or whatever's a step up from terrific!"

The sergeant chuckled. "It is a bit of all right. You can outturn a German in a 109 and get on his tail. And a Spitfire's as fast as a Messerschmitt on the level, too, which a Hurricane isn't." He paused.

"But?" she prompted. "Whenever somebody stops like that, there's always a but."

"There is. A 109 can outclimb you, and outdive you, too," the veteran said. "If Jerry comes at you from above and behind, you're in trouble. And if he's in trouble, he'll dive away from you and you can't catch him. A 109 has fuel injection. It doesn't hiccup in steep dives or climbs the way a carburetor does."

"I'll remember," A.E. said.

By the way the sergeant's eyebrow quirked, he had his doubts. "You'd better," he said, "or your people back home will get a telegram they don't want."

She'd flown into danger before. If Fred Noonan hadn't found Howland Island before the Lockheed Electra ran out of gas, the ocean would have swallowed the plane and left never a trace. But that kind of danger was impersonal, the inevitable result of natural circumstances. The men in the plane with the swastikas on their tails would be trying to kill her.

Air combat seemed a lot less romantic when you

looked at it that way. From above and behind, the RAF sergeant had said. A fighter plane was nothing but a fancy, expensive tool for sneaking up on another pilot and shooting him in the back—before he could do the same to you.

# CHAPTER SEVEN

---

BY THE END OF JULY, the apprentice pilots at Croydon OTU had learned what they could there. A.E. knew she'd done better than most of the men. She also knew the RAF powers that be were liable to wash her out anyway, for no better reason than that she had to squat when she took a leak.

But they didn't. Things in the air were getting more desperate by the day. Even the RAF brass could see they needed every man, and even woman, they could find who had half a notion how to fly a fighter plane. Along with Shorty, Andy, and Red, she got posted to 609 Squadron at Middle Wallop, a little north and east of Salisbury and Stonehenge.

Before the pilots who'd trained together went to their squadrons, they threw a last bash. As Red Tobin said afterwards, it got pretty drunk out. *Eat, drink, and be merry!* seemed uppermost in everybody's mind. A.E.

remembered that that phrase had another part, too. No one came out and said *For tomorrow we die!*, but it seemed to be on more people's minds than hers alone.

She drank less than most of the men did. For one thing, she was the oldest person in the training group. She'd just turned forty-three; one fellow was thirty-eight, a few more in their early thirties, but most of the men ranged from eighteen to twenty-five. For another, she never had enjoyed getting smashed for the sake of getting smashed. And, for one more, a woman with any sense didn't get loaded with a bunch of young men.

She knew them all. She was going to trust some of them with her life, and they'd trust her with theirs. All of which had nothing to do with the price of beer ... or wine, or scotch.

A South African she'd called Pete for a while before finding out he spelled it Piet slipped an arm around her and tried to kiss her. She didn't kiss him back, which was one of the points to staying within shouting distance of sober. He scowled and gave her a reproachful stare. "What's the matter with you?" he said, his accent sounding almost German in her ears.

"Nothing's the matter with me. What's the matter with you?" she replied. "I'm old enough to be your mother." She wasn't kidding in the least; his spotty face said he couldn't have been much above twenty-one.

"My mother doesn't look like you," he said, and tried again. This time, he put a hand against the back of her head so he could mash her mouth against his.

But she knew what to do about that. She'd long since lost track of how many would-be wolves she'd dealt with over the years. A woman both good-looking and famous drew them the way a sirloin drew hungry hounds.

Instead of trying to pull away from his tug, she went with it. Not at all by accident, her forehead hit the bridge of his nose, hard. He yowled like a cat with its tail under a rocking chair. He also let go of her so he could clap both hands to the injured part.

They came away bloody. More blood ran over his mouth and chin. "You filthy bitch! You meant to do that!" he said thickly.

"Damn right, I did," A.E. said. "I told you I wasn't interested. Didn't you think I meant it?"

"I ought to—" Instead of going on, Piet made a fist.

Before he could do whatever he was going do to, a large hand came down on his shoulder. "Leave the lady alone, shithead, or I'll make you sorry," Red Tobin said evenly.

Piet growled something that wasn't English and didn't sound like an endearment. Then he added, "You and who else?"

"I'm the who else." Andy appeared behind Red.

"Me, too." So did Shorty Keough, though you had to look hard to find him.

Piet's bloody nose did nothing to improve his scowl. "Screw you all," he said, and stamped away.

"Thanks, boys, but you didn't have to do that. I can take care of myself," A.E. said. The next step after the butt to the nose was the knee to the nuts. She didn't believe in fair fights with anyone who thought she was nothing but a nicely shaped toy.

"We didn't do it because we had to. We did it because we wanted to," Shorty said.

"You bet." Andy Mamedoff nodded emphatically. "Going after the Nazis is bad enough. You shouldn't have to take on guys who say they're on your side, too."

"Thanks," A.E. said again, this time with more warmth. She'd known the Yanks put up with her, even if they thought she was crazy for wanting to fly fighters. Till this moment, she hadn't been sure they actually liked her. How much knowing that meant amazed her.

RED TOBIN promptly nicknamed Middle Wallop "Center Punch." He and the other two American men were quartered in the barracks with the other male pilots. Flight Officer Darley, the squadron commander, proposed billeting A.E. with the WAAF personnel at the other end of the airfield.

"Sir, if there's a scramble on I may not hear it in time and I may not be able to get to my kite fast enough if you do that." A.E. was picking up the RAF lingo.

"You're serious about this," Darley said slowly.

"Would I be here if I weren't ... sir?"

The pause before the honorific made him send her a

sharp look. She stared back steadily. "What do you suggest, then?" he asked.

"Every time I wind up at a base, they stick me in a tent. That's okay. I don't mind."

"You won't like it so well once winter comes on."

"If I'm still here in winter, we can worry about it then."

Darley took *If I'm still here* exactly the way she'd meant it. This time, his examination struck her as measuring. "Quite," he murmured, and then, "Well, let it be as you say."

For her first couple of weeks at the base she got ferry duty, taking Spitfires to other bases where they were needed and coming back in a Miles Master or some other two-seater. Since Shorty, Red, and Andy drew the same kind of assignments, she didn't complain. And every hour in a plane she was still learning did her good.

Sure as the devil, the Germans kept hitting England, and particularly RAF bases, harder and harder. Middle Wallop took a walloping. A.E. had just landed in a trainer when Ju 88s appeared overhead and started unloading bombs.

She stood frozen for a moment. Red's warning shout unfroze her in a hurry. She dashed for a trench by the runway, and dove into it just before the bombs started bursting.

The roar, the blast like a slap in the face, dirt pattering down on her from a couple of near misses ... This was combat, combat when you couldn't shoot back.

The war suddenly felt less abstract, more personal. Those Nazi sons of bitches were trying to murder her! She wanted the chance to pay them back.

Red Tobin popped up from another trench not far away. He didn't seem to notice he was wearing a good-sized chunk of dirt in his hair, the way a pretty girl might wear a flower. Grinning at A.E., he said, "Wow! That was fun!"

"Now that you mention it," she answered tightly, "no." Despite her effort to control her voice, it wobbled. She felt as she would have after a crash landing she managed to come out of unhurt. You always felt the consciousness of disaster when you flew. Sometimes you felt it like a slap in the face. This was one of *those* times.

She got her first chance for revenge a few days later, when the squadron CO declared her and the other three Yanks "operational." She wasn't sure she liked that; it sounded as if they were new bits of machinery bolted on to the RAF.

She also wasn't sure she liked the job they got handed. RAF fighters flew in vics of three: a leader and two wingmen. Two vics made a flight; two flights made a squadron. The nice, neat—to A.E.'s mind, rigid—squadron needed a couple of extra planes weaving along behind to keep an eye peeled for trouble from the rear and above.

"Tail-end Charlie, that's me." Andy Mamedoff sounded more cheerful than he looked.

"That's all of us," Shorty Keough said. Plainly, when

you were buzzing around by yourself your chances were worse than they would have been with friends close by. If you lived for a while, you'd graduate to a spot in the formation. If you didn't, somebody else would get a chance ... till the limeys ran out of somebody elses, anyhow.

They went into action the next day. Before they did, Flight Lieutenant Darley spoke to his pilots in the crowded little wardroom. "I want you all to take a good look around. Most of the men sitting here with you will be dead a year from now."

The charming Air Vice Marshal Leigh-Mallory had told A.E. much the same thing. No American would have. Americans always were, or at least acted, sure they could come through anything. Englishmen took a grimmer, or maybe just a more realistic, view of the world.

"Those Nazi bastards are going to try to knock England flat," the squadron leader went on. "We'll do our damnedest not to let them. Good luck, one and all! Let's go to the planes."

They scrambled several times that day, but never got airborne. As the sun finally set that evening—England lay so far north, summer days seemed to stretch like taffy —A.E. didn't know whether to be disappointed or relieved.

One of the genuine Englishmen in the squadron, a pilot who'd seen a lot of action in France and over the Channel, had no doubts on that score. "Any day they aren't shooting at you, my dear, is a bloody good day, and you may take it to the bank," he told her.

*My dear* grated a little; he wouldn't have said that to Andy or Shorty or Red. But he would have called them *old chap* or *old boy* or something like that. She decided it wasn't worth fussing about. Next to burning in the cockpit like a rump roast forgotten in the oven or taking a bullet or a shell fragment in the leg or in the face, it didn't seem so bad. You had to pick your fights. She'd picked hers, by God.

The squadron did go into action the next day. The Yanks alternated on rear-guard duties. A.E. would have flown before; that day, it was Red and Andy's turn. Andy barely made it back to the base. A 109 had shot up his Spitfire from behind. The plane had been elderly when he got it, and was a write-off now.

He wasn't a write-off himself for one reason only: his armored seat back had just about kept a couple of 20mm shells from getting through. The steel was dented; Andy Mamedoff's back wasn't ... quite. He got out of the cockpit as if he'd suddenly aged fifty years, and went on hobbling after his boots hit the grass.

"I bet I'm all bruised up back there," he said. "Felt like somebody hauled off and slammed me with a Louisville Slugger."

"With a what?" asked a groundcrew man who didn't speak American.

"A baseball bat," Mamedoff explained. "But I never saw the son of a gun"—he winked at A.E.—"till he opened up on me. I was flying along, getting ready to make a run at one of the Stukas over the Channel, and then—*wham!* After that, I was just praying I wouldn't have to ditch."

"Glad you're here," A.E. told him.

He winked at her. "You ain't half as glad as I am, believe you me you ain't."

## CHAPTER EIGHT

THEY FLEW DOWN TO WARMWELL, Middle Wallop's forward air base, the next day. Warmwell lay south and west of Middle Wallop: just inland from the coast, a few miles west of Bournemouth. Middle Wallop was a little English country town. Next to a city like Salisbury, it was nothing much. Next to Warmwell, it could have been London.

A.E. had a tent, and in it she lived distinctly better than the men of the squadron did in their squalid barracks. Plumbing arrangements there left everything to be desired. Instead of using them, the men stepped into the bushes by the path to spend a penny. That was less convenient for her, so she endured the odorous facilities.

The flyers wanted breakfast as soon as it got light. They knew the Germans would be out and about early themselves. Civilian cooks resented getting up at three in the morning to fix bacon and eggs for the men defending the skies. They resented it so much, they flat-out refused to do it.

Left to their own devices, the pilots scorched things on their Primus stoves. Flight Lieutenant Darley quietly asked A.E., "Can you do any better than they are?"

She shook her head. "Sorry, sir. I'm a much better pilot than I am a cook. I'll eat whatever they make, and I won't grouse about it."

Muttering under his breath, the squadron CO slouched off. A.E. let out a silent sigh of relief that he hadn't chosen to push it. She'd told him a white lie. No one would ever accuse her of being a great cook, but she knew she outclassed her male squadronmates. But she also knew Darley'd only asked her because she was a woman. She was damned if she'd slave at a stove for no better reason than that.

She was flying tail-end Charlie when the squadron went up to protect a convoy moving east through the Channel. And the convoy needed protecting; *Luftwaffe* bombers, escorted by 109s and 110s, came north from France to harry it.

A 110's rear gunner opened up on her. She returned fire: eight machine guns hitting back at one. One of the enemy heavy fighter's engines began to smoke. It pulled away and fled back towards its base. She put more bullets into it, and it spun down, out of control.

Then she was dogfighting with a pair of 109s, and glad to break away when she could. The Germans didn't

fly in rigid vics. They had pairs: a leader and his wingman. Sometimes two of those pairs would fly together to
protect each other. That seemed a lot more flexible than
the RAF approach.

Before long, the German bomber pilots decided they
weren't going to be able to unload on that convoy after
all. They turned around and headed for France again.
Their escorts followed. "Let's go home," Flight Lieutenant Darley said. A.E. didn't think she'd ever heard
such welcome words in her earphones.

She felt ... She didn't know how she felt. Like a
freshly washed dress that had just gone through the
wringer—she couldn't come any closer. She didn't seem
to own any bones. Why she didn't ooze out of the seat
and puddle on the cockpit floor, she couldn't have said.

She remembered to lower the landing gear before
she touched down. After bouncing to a stop, she opened
the canopy, undid her harness, and climbed out. The
first thing she saw, now that the prop wasn't spinning
any more, was that one blade had a bullet hole. The Spitfire had taken another hit on the left wing, and—she
looked back—a couple of more in the fuselage. The
Germans had been playing for keeps.

Well, so had she. Her squadron mates came running
up, shouting congratulations. "You did for that one
bugger—I saw him go in!"

"The way you got clear of those 109s! Like a water-
melon seed squirting out between their fingers!"

She hopped down to the ground. Her legs barely

held her upright. A couple of men wanted to pound her on the back. She shook them off, stumbled around behind the Spit's far wheel, bent over, and was noisily sick on the grass. There'd been two young men in that Messerschmitt 110. They'd never see their parents or their wives and children—if they had any—again.

She'd killed them, was what she'd done.

Someone set a hand on her shoulder. She started to twist away. "Hold on," the squadron CO said. "I did the same thing after I shot down my first Jerry in France. You can rinse your mouth with this, if you care to." He held out a small, silvered flask, the kind you might have seen at a college football game during Prohibition.

"Thanks," A.E. managed, and took a swig. She swished it around, then spat. "Shame to do that to such good brandy."

"Sometimes you need it," Darley said. "If you want to swallow the next one, that's all right, too." She did. The brandy slid down her throat, smooth and fiery at the same time.

"Thanks," she said again, coughing only a little at the end of the word.

"And if you care to come to the pub tonight and hoist a few, sometimes you need that, too." Darley's smile was the more charming for being a bit crooked. "One thing you'll find in a hurry is that oxygen and raw fear make sovereign hangover cures."

"I don't think I want to do that right now, but we'll see for sure later on," A.E. replied. He nodded and left it there. Even if he had thought she ought to cook for the squadron along with flying her missions, he made a pretty fair CO.

ONE DAY IN EARLY SEPTEMBER, Shorty and Red got leave to go into London. They'd heard Colonel Sweeny was in town at last. Neither they, Andy, nor A.E. had yet to see a franc, a shilling, or even a good old American nickel for their time in France. Red and Shorty hoped to pry some dough out of him.

A.E. didn't worry about it so much. She wasn't rich, but she was a long way from poor. Books and swings on the lecture circuit had let her cash in on her flying fame. Now that she wasn't married to George Putnam any more, her expenses were down; he'd liked living well. And the post at Purdue she'd left to join the RAF brought in nice, regular paychecks. She hadn't known those since abandoning social work for flight in 1928.

She understood she was luckier than the young men with whom she'd crossed the Atlantic. They needed anything they could get their hands on, since a pilot officer's pay was a whopping £16 a month, which came to just over $67. Of course, pilot officers' privileges also included room, board, and the daily chance to get killed.

And, if you were a Yank in the RAF, they included talking with the press, too. After her first kill, A.E. had given interviews to God only knew how many English reporters. When Edward R. Murrow saw the stories, she'd spoken with him on the radio, shortwave carrying her words across the ocean to the States.

She wasn't a natural performer, but she'd done enough of it to know how. And she knew every word she said helped bring other American flyers to England to join the fight against the Nazis. Her fame and her sex were part of the reason Colonel Sweeny had been so keen to bring her to Europe to begin with.

BACK AT MIDDLE WALLOP AGAIN, the morning was quiet but nervous. The *Luftwaffe* had started bombing London instead of RAF airfields a couple of days before, and England had replied with a night air raid on Berlin. How Hitler would respond to high explosives raining down on his capital ... was why the base was quiet but nervous.

The scramble came a little before 1600. "They're hitting London with everything they've got this time!" Flight Lieutenant Darley called as the pilots ran to their planes.

A.E. knew the RAF had some fancy, supersecret, radio-related way to detect incoming German planes far out of range of eye and ear. She hadn't asked about the details. Curiosity about such things was not encouraged. What you didn't know, you couldn't spill if you got shot down over the Channel or France and the enemy captured you.

She and Andy were going to play tail-end Charlie again. Neither one of them grumbled about it. They were heading into action ... and, if they stayed lucky, it wasn't likely everyone else would. Sooner or later, they'd be veterans with regular slots in a vic, and some fresh-faced kid just out of OTU would weave around behind trying to keep them safe.

Middle Wallop lay seventy-five miles west of London —fifteen minutes in a Spitfire. Long before she got there, A.E. saw pillars of smoke rising from the greatest city in the world. Somewhere over there, Shorty and Red were having their palaver with Charles Sweeny. She hoped they'd be all right. After a moment, she hoped Sweeny would, too.

As she drew closer, she saw the sky over London filled with planes: bombers, some still in formation, others scattered, dropping their cargo of death; and fighters both German and British darting this way and that, some attacking the bombers, others trying to hold the attackers at bay. Every antiaircraft gun for miles around was firing for all it was worth. Puffs of black smoke with flame at their heart punctuated the chaos.

When an antiaircraft shell burst near her plane, the Spitfire bounced in the air like a car with bad shocks hitting a pothole. She hadn't thought her own side might shoot her down by mistake. She shrugged. She couldn't do anything about it if they did.

As soon as the bombers unloaded, they ran for France as fast as they could go. That often wasn't fast enough. RAF doctrine was for Spitfires to engage the *Luftwaffe* escorts while Hurricanes went after the bombers. Hurricanes weren't quite up to matching 109s: not hopeless against them, but at a disadvantage.

A.E. quickly found doctrine flew out the window when you were up there trying to stay alive. She fired a short burst at a Do 17. The Flying Pencil kept flying, so either she missed or the Dornier was good at soaking up damage.

Then tracers flew past her own plane. She swung the stick as hard to the left as she could. G-forces almost made her gray out for a moment. Unwisely, the German on her tail tried to turn with her. A 109 might outclimb or outdive a Spit, but the British fighter turned more tightly. All of a sudden, she was on the Jerry's tail, not the other way around.

She thumbed the red firing button. From this range, she could hardly miss—and she didn't. Chunks of aluminum skin flew off the 109. Belching first smoke and then fire, it went into a long, spinning dive. She didn't see the pilot hit the silk.

When her fuel ran low, she headed back to Middle Wallop. "Gas me up quick as you can and give me more ammo," she told the groundcrew men who ran over to her plane. "I've got to head back. They're still giving London hell."

"How'd you do this time, ma'am?" a corporal asked.

"Got one—a 109," she said.

"Good on you!" he said. One of his crewmates gave her a thumbs-up. Grinning, she returned it.

She closed the cockpit, fired up the Spit's Merlin, and bounced along the airstrip till she got airborne. As she pulled back the stick to gain altitude, she realized that what some of the older hands had said after her first victory was true.

The second time you killed somebody, you didn't feel a thing.

# CHAPTER NINE

THE NEXT FEW days went by in a blur, exhaustion tempered by moments of raw terror. She lost track of how many sorties she flew. So did the men she flew with. They didn't even have time to shave, and got scruffier by the day.

"Where's *your* beard, Pilot Officer Earhart?" the squadron CO demanded with mock ferocity when they both happened to be on the ground at the same time.

"Sorry, sir. I forget where I left it," A.E. answered. Flight Lieutenant Darley laughed more than the comeback deserved. If he was as worn as she was, he had no business being upright and functional.

Other pilots in the squadron had made kills, too. And three of them had got shot down themselves. One bailed out and came back to Middle Wallop with no worse than a limp from an ankle he'd twisted on landing. The other two bought a plot when their Spits went down, dying either from German gunfire or in the crash.

Victories and deaths were observed the same way: with frenzied drinking at Middle Wallop's pubs and with equally frenzied screwing with whatever willing women the flyers could find. A.E. stayed in her tent after it got too dark to fly one more mission. Unlike Achilles, she wasn't sulking there. She just didn't want to cramp her friends' style. If they'd found ways to unwind, to forget for a little while what they did, more power to them.

For a solid week, the Germans poured everything they had into wrecking London and the RAF. The consensus in 609 Squadron was that they'd also gone a long way toward wrecking the *Luftwaffe*.

"They can't go on like this," Red Tobin said as he bolted supper before heading out for whatever debaucheries Middle Wallop had on offer. "They'll run out of planes and crews. They don't buy anything cheap there, any more than anybody else does."

"Will we have anything left when they pack it in?" A.E. only wished the question were rhetorical.

Red shrugged and ran a comb through his hair. Yes, he had other things on his mind than grand military strategy, things he could actually do something about. "Beats me," he said cheerfully. "As long as we've got one Spit—or even a Hurricane—flying when fat old Göring runs dry, we win, right?"

Like jesting Pilate, the jesting pilot didn't wait for an

answer. He hopped on a bicycle and pedaled off to the raucous nightlife of Middle Wallop.

A.E. stood on the grass, watching him shrink in the distance. Twilight hadn't left the sky. No sooner had she thought she wouldn't care to fly so near darkness than she heard an airplane motor. Someone up there was trying it—a German far off course or somebody from the RAF looking for a place to set down.

She turned her head, trying to spot the aircraft by the direction its sound came from. She still had pretty good ears. Sometimes that surprised her, given how much time she'd spent too close to roaring airplane engines. Surprise or not, it was true.

And sure enough, she did pick up the plane before it came in and landed at the Middle Wallop airstrip. Not a lost *Luftwaffe* pilot—it was a Westland Lysander, a two-seater the RAF used for everything from trainer to ground attack. Very early in the war, one had shot down a Heinkel bomber, though Lysanders carried only a pair of forward-facing machine guns when they mounted any at all.

One other thing Lysanders did a lot of was serve as glorified taxis. If an officer of suitably exalted rank needed to go somewhere far away in a hurry, he'd hop in a Lysander. Either he'd fly it himself or a pilot would whisk him to his destination.

That seemed to be what was going on here. An RAF officer got out of the plane and made for the battered bungalow that was optimistically called the ops shack. A moment later, the pilot came down to the ground, too, and stepped away from the Lysander, wanting a stretch or maybe a cigarette.

A.E. ambled over toward the pilot. "Your passenger won't find whoever he's looking for in there," she said. "Everybody but me's in town, trying to blot out everything they've done today."

Her American accent and, she realized a beat slower than she might have, her contralto made the pilot snap her head up sharply and ask, "Who the devil are you?" She was a woman, too.

Automatically, A.E. answered, "Pilot Officer Earhart, 609 Squadron. Who are *you*?"

The other pilot burst out laughing. She was several inches shorter than A.E., though several inches taller than Shorty Keough. "Oh, good Lord, this is too mad for words!" she said. As A.E. realized her voice sounded not just feminine but familiar, she went on, "That I should land at the airfield where you're stationed when I stayed in your house in New York!"

A.E.'s eyes widened. "My God, Amy Johnson!" She squeezed the English aviatrix. They'd met before that in London, when A.E. was the first woman to fly solo across the Atlantic. Amy and her then-husband tried to duplicate the crossing going the other way, but crashed on landing; he was hurt worse than she was.

And now both women were still flying, but neither was still married. They'd loved planes before they met their spouses, and kept loving them though their spouses were spouses no more.

That was bound to mean something. Before A.E. could begin to work out what, Amy Johnson's passenger came back toward the Lysander. "Where in damnation has Flight Lieutenant Darley got to?" he demanded, as if expecting A.E. to have the squadron CO in her back pocket.

"Sir, he and just about all the other flyers have gone into town to take the edge off the day's fighting," she said.

"Except for you? Who the devil are you?" the officer unwittingly echoed the woman who'd flown him here.

"I'm Pilot Officer Earhart, sir," A.E. said, as she had to Amy Johnson. She didn't ask him who he was. Englishmen were touchier than Yanks about rank.

"Oh," the RAF man said. "I've heard of you, yes. Jolly good, what you're doing—*jolly* good. But how do I get to Middle Wallop?"

He could have walked; it was only a couple of miles from the airbase. He'd taken A.E.'s anomalous gender and rank in stride, though, or better than in stride. Because he had, she said, "You can borrow my bicycle if you like, sir. It's a man's bike—no one will laugh at you for riding a girl's machine."

"That's white of you! Much obliged, Pilot Officer. I promise I'll bring it back in good shape," the officer said. A.E. led him and Amy Johnson over to her tent. The man thanked her again and rode away. A.E. had no idea whether anyone could distract Darley from drinking and wenching. The newly come officer might have a headache or a drippy faucet tomorrow. That wasn't A.E.'s worry, though.

As soon as the fellow had gone a couple of hundred yards, Amy Johnson spoke in a low voice. "I'm so jealous of you I could spit, Amelia."

"Of me? What did I do?"

"You shot down a couple of German planes, that's what!" the Englishwoman said fiercely. "I'm stuck ferrying important people—important *men*, don't you know?—from yon to hither, or taking planes where they need to go next. It stinks!" She kicked at the dirt in frustration.

"Why *aren't* you in the RAF instead of the WAAF?" A.E. asked. "God knows you've got more experience and more sense than some of the half-trained guys they're sticking in Spitfires."

"They won't let me. I'm not an American coming over here with a boatload of press cuttings and an appetite for more. I'm just ... part of the scenery, is all I am." Amy Johnson didn't try to hide her bitterness.

A.E. nodded toward her elegant accommodations. "C'mon in. Let's talk. I've got most of a quart of scotch in there. Andy Mamedoff—he's one of the fellas who came over with me—gave it to me in case I needed to unwind the way the guys do. I haven't touched it till now, but this looks like a pretty good time."

"I should have flown back to Norwich," Amy said

doubtfully. But then she nodded. "Why not? They can't be browned off at me—it *was* dark by the time I got here."

They ducked into the tent together. It was crowded for two, but not impossibly so. A.E. made sure the flap was secured before she lit the kerosene lamp—only it was a paraffin lamp over here—that sat on a camp stool. She fished out the scotch and perched awkwardly on the cot next to Amy; with the lamp on the stool, it was the only place she could sit.

She poured some of the amber fluid into her tin cup, then handed Amy the bottle. "Mud in your eye," she said, and clinked tin against glass.

Amy coughed. She made as if to read the label: "'Aged in oaken barrels for at least twenty minutes.'" Then she sipped again as A.E. laughed. She added, "It may not be good, but it's strong."

"Genuine paint thinner," A.E. agreed. Then she came back to what they'd talked about outside. "Seriously, if you want to fly fighters, you ought to go see Leigh-Mallory or Sholto Douglas or one of the other RAF big shots and raise a stink. Nothing ever happens if you don't make a stink about it."

"The only thing that would happen is they'd throw me out of the WAAF on my ear," Amy said. "This isn't the USA. They don't much fancy stinks over here." She drank some more.

"Hey, save some for me!" A.E. held out the cup. Amy poured more of the cheap scotch into it. A.E. went on, "Do you want me to go in to London with you? If the people who run the RAF don't have a damn good reason for keeping a pilot like you out, we can tell the papers all about it."

"I'm game, but it won't do any good," Amy said glumly. "Men can be such bastards sometimes. A lot of the time, in fact."

"Ain't that the truth!" A.E. said, remembering her tiff with Air Vice Marshal Leigh-Mallory. She remembered other things, too. "I heard you and Jim broke up."

The Englishwoman nodded. "Afraid so. We couldn't make it go any more, so we finally quit trying. Better than cutting each other up all the bloody time. You and your George aren't husband and wife any more, either, are you?"

"Nope." A.E. shook her head. "George always had a roving eye. He dumped somebody else to get together with me, and he married somebody new right after our divorce went final." She chuckled. Was she feeling the scotch? Oh, maybe a little. "Of course, my eye roves, too, I guess. I wrote the agreement we signed before we tied the knot, and one of the things it said was we didn't have to be faithful that way to each other."

Amy drank some more. Then she poured some more into A.E.'s cup. And then she let the bottle fall to the ground. Between them, they were going to kill it. Maybe it was just the dim light from the kerosene lamp, but her eyes looked enormous. She said, "You know, I've always admired you so much. From the very first moment we met, I have."

"Me? That's just silly." A.E. drained what was in the cup. She hardly even felt it going down. And she understood why the men in the squadron drank so hard after every run-in with the Jerries. Booze helped shield you from the slings and arrows and machine-gun bullets and 20mm shells of outrageous fortune. She tried to remember what she'd been talking about. With almost as much triumph as she'd felt shooting down her second German plane, she did. "I'm nobody special."

"Oh, but you are!" Amy sounded very sure of herself, which was also bound to be the rotgut talking. "You always seem to take everything in stride. And the university work you've done, the aeronautical research. And you started doing things for women long before you came over here and put on the uniform. Compared to you, I always thought I flew for myself."

"No better reason," A.E. said. If oxygen and adrenaline *didn't* kill her hangover tomorrow morning, she was going to feel like grim death. The tip of her nose had gone numb, a warning of how much she'd put away.

"You're sweet to say so." Amy slid closer on the cot and put an arm around her.

It seemed the most natural thing in the world for A.E. to kiss her on the cheek. Only her aim, thanks to the scotch, wasn't all it might have been. The kiss, to her surprise, landed square on Amy's mouth. The way Amy kissed her back was a surprise, too. So was how much she liked it.

Not very much later, she blew out the lamp. Even while it was going on, she had the feeling that what happened there in the quiet darkness might not be quite real. If *We were drunk* wasn't the oldest excuse in the world, she couldn't imagine what would be.

But it was pretty wonderful while it went on. Yes, the scotch helped. So did the jangle of nerves that had brushed too close to death's black wing. When you were with someone else, you could forget about that for a little while. Again, she understood her comrades-in-arms better.

Afterwards, she did. At the time, she just enjoyed it. "Well," Amy said softly as their hearts slowed together, "I never looked for *that* to happen."

"Neither did I," A.E. said, and then, "Officially, of course, it never did."

"Right." Amy giggled, still in a tiny voice. "Bound to be against regulations, don't you know?"

A.E. laughed so hard, she had to hold her face to the rough, scratchy RAF blanket to muffle the noise. It wasn't even that Amy was wrong. This was bound to be against a whole raft of regulations. That only made it funnier. "We'd better put ourselves back together."

When they were more or less decent again, she lit the lamp once more so they could get the details right. "What do we do now?" Amy asked.

"Let's go to bed," A.E. said. The Englishwoman

looked at her. "To sleep, I mean," she amended. "We've both got to fly tomorrow, and we need what rest we can grab."

"I told you you were sensible," Amy said. Her flying jacket, which she hadn't bothered putting back on, lay on the yellowing grass by the cot. A.E. saw it had a grease stain and a tear. It belonged to a working pilot, and had seen hard use. Why didn't the RAF understand that, dammit?

The cot was narrow for one. It was very narrow for two, no matter how friendly they were. A.E. didn't care. As soon as darkness returned, she fell asleep as if clubbed.

# CHAPTER TEN

A.E. HAD LOST the habit of waking up with someone else in bed with her. She'd never got into the habit of waking up with someone else in bed draped all over her. That her head pounded like her Spitfire's machine guns added nothing to the experience.

"Morning," Amy Johnson said, her mouth maybe three inches from A.E.'s ear.

"It is, isn't it?" A.E. agreed sorrowfully. Amy seemed no more chipper than she was, which pleased her as much as anything was likely to just then.

They untangled from each other. A.E. found a little tin of aspirins and took three. Amy held out her hand. A.E. gave her three, too.

Some of the men were already tucking into breakfast when they walked in together. Eggs were in short supply in England these days, but not for RAF flyers. When A.E. introduced her companion, a considerable silence fell. Red Tobin broke it. "My God! Between the two of you, you've done about everything a pilot can do."

"We haven't shot down enough Germans yet," A.E. said, a remark that met general approval.

Shorty eyed Amy Johnson. "How come *you're* not in a Spitfire instead of playing shuttle pilot? Any damn fool can do that."

"Because the RAF brass are a bunch of dodoes," A.E. said before Amy could reply.

Hot tea (A.E. would rather have had coffee, but what could you do?) and greasy food helped the aspirins blunt her hangover. Amy also looked more lifelike when she walked out to the Lysander. "This was more interesting than I thought it would be when I landed here," she said, scrambling up into the cockpit.

"I don't know what you could mean," A.E. answered, deadpan. They both laughed. If A.E.'s chuckles sounded self-conscious in her own ears, she had good enough reason for that. She hadn't looked for what had happened to happen, either. It didn't feel sinful, the way she'd half wondered if it would—more just one of the crazy things war could bring on. She continued, "When the Germans let up, if they ever do, we'll go into London and browbeat the RAF."

"If you want to. You don't have to." Amy was less inclined to rock the boat than A.E. was. Maybe that was the difference between England and the USA.

"I want to," A.E. said firmly. *If I'm still alive* went through her head. She gave a kind of mental shrug. She worried about that much less than she'd ever thought she would. You couldn't brood. You'd buy a plot for sure if you did.

"Back to business as usual for now. Stand well clear of the prop, if you please—you know the drill," Amy said before closing the cockpit. A.E. nodded and stepped away. She *did* know the drill, and knew a spinning prop would take your head off like a guillotine.

The Lysander's engine rumbled to life. It was a half-pint next to a Spitfire's powerplant, but plenty noisy enough for all ordinary use. Just before Amy started taxiing away, she blew A.E. a kiss. A.E. returned it. That was probably against regulations, too, unless it hadn't occurred to the regulation writers that two flyers might do such a thing.

After a sedate takeoff run, the Army co-op plane hopped into the air and buzzed away. A.E. watched it go for a little while, then looked around. The base at Middle Wallop seemed duller than it had before.

As she slowly walked back to her tent, Andy Mamedoff came up to her and said, "Boy, you know all kinds of interesting people, don't you?"

"Sure. I know you, for instance." A.E. looked him up and down.

"Ha!" he snorted. "I mean people who've done stuff, people other people've heard of. You know—people like you."

"Oh, cut it out. The only thing I want to do is shoot down more Germans and not let them get me."

"Amen! You listening, God? You better be listening!" Andy raised his eyes to the heavens, as if to see whether God *was* paying attention.

A.E. didn't quite get shot down that afternoon, but her Spit got shot up. As Andy had before her, she came to appreciate the virtues of an armored seat back. Hers stopped machine-gun rounds, not cannon shells, so she didn't get anywhere near so badly bruised as he had. Even so, she knew she'd fly a different plane tomorrow. This one needed some patching up.

So did 609 Squadron. One of the other pilots had less luck or skill than she did, which meant the squadron had another slot to fill. Flight Lieutenant Darley held his head in his hands at dinner that evening. "I *hate* writing these letters of condolence," he said to no one in particular. "'So sorry, my dear, but you'll never see your husband again. He was clever, he was brave, he's dead.' Ralph had only been married six months. His wife is expecting, I think."

Again, A.E. wondered whether the RAF or the *Luft-waffe* would run out of fighter pilots first. That was the only thing that mattered in the war right now. If the RAF ran out, the *Luftwaffe* would knock London flat and the *Wehrmacht* would invade. If the *Luftwaffe* couldn't stand the gaff ... England had some kind of chance, anyhow.

The Germans kept trying to smash London and take the RAF out of the fight till the fifteenth. Then, grudgingly, their daylight attacks tapered off. A.E. noticed more slowly than it happened. She noticed much more that she was weary unto death and half stunned at having survived when so many didn't.

Sometime toward the end of the month, she sent Amy Johnson a wire suggesting they meet in London to beard the RAF in its den. The reply took a couple of days to reach her. She wondered how far around the country her telegram had chased Amy before finally catching her.

They needed some more finagling after the agreement, too. Finding a day when they could both get off duty wasn't easy. Easy or not, they managed. "Yes, you can go," Darley told A.E. "You ask for so little, it sometimes worries me."

"There's a war on, sir," she said.

He managed a laugh of sorts. "Yes, I'd noticed. Go on, before anything happens that really reminds me of it."

SHE'D BEEN in London before the Blitz began. Stepping off the train now was like stepping into another world, or perhaps into one of the shabbier parts of hell. Piles of bricks where buildings had been, empty lots where buildings had been, buildings with chunks bitten out of them, the stink of sour smoke, the fainter but unmistakable stink of death some time past but not yet uncovered and cleaned up ... The greatest city the world had ever known had taken the greatest pounding the world had ever seen.

And the Londoners remained cheekily defiant. "'E'll 'ave to do better than *that* if 'e wants to knock us off-kilter," A.E. heard one cloth-capped workman tell another on her bus ride to RAF headquarters.

Amy waited outside. A.E. was in trousers; Amy wore a skirt. Their uniforms had other differences that marked one of them as the genuine article and the other as that lukewarm thing, an auxiliary.

"We'll get in trouble," Amy said as they walked into the not too battered building.

"The Germans want to kill me. What can the RAF do that's worse?" A.E. asked.

All Amy said was, "You'll find out."

The first thing the RAF tried to do was throw her out without listening to her. She said no. She kept saying no. The flunkies trying to get rid of her were underofficers. She had on her pilot officer's uniform, with her pilot's wings prominently displayed. The sergeant-bureaucrats finally booted her up to a flight lieutenant.

"You're being unreasonable," he said.

"No, sir," she said. "I've shot down two German fighters, probably damaged some others, and certainly scared bombers away. Amy Johnson is at least as good a pilot as I am. She's younger and likely faster. Why shouldn't she have a chance to defend her country?"

"She's a woman," he said, as if to an idiot.

"So am I ... sir. Planes don't care who flies them.

Bullets don't care who shoots them. It's not about men and women. It's about good pilots and bad ones. Amy Johnson's as good as you're gonna get. Years ago, in Los Angeles, I made a speech where I said women ought to be called up to serve alongside men. I still think so."

"You're an American. You don't understand how these things work."

"You're here. We're here. Hitler's over there." A.E. pointed south, past the English Channel toward France. "Amy can help keep him over there and not let him come over here. What else do I need to understand?"

He turned red. Then he picked up a telephone. When he put it down again, he said, "I'm sending you to Air Marshal Douglas's office, on the third floor. If he wants to listen to you, he will. If he wants to clap you in irons, he'll do that." By the way he sounded, he hoped the air marshal would.

A.E. saluted. "Thank you, sir." She ignored his tone.

As they went up the stairs, Amy said, "You're wonderful. You're quite insane, but you're wonderful."

"You say the sweetest things," A.E. answered. They both laughed.

They had to cool their heels in Sholto Douglas's outer office before being ushered into his presence. He was nearing fifty, a bit fleshy, but with a crack fighter pilot's deadly stare. The first thing he said was, "I can give you five minutes." The next was, "I don't like Americans one bit. You're an undisciplined lot, and you revel in it."

"Thank you, sir," A.E. said again, which made him blink. Then she told him the same thing she'd told the flight lieutenant downstairs.

He let her finish. Then he said, "No. Get out."

She saluted again and left, Amy following in her wake. As soon as the door closed behind them, Amy said, "I told you that would happen."

"Yeah, you did," A.E. agreed cheerfully. "Now we go talk to the newspapers."

Amy looked worried. "He really may clap us in irons for that."

"How can he? He never ordered us not to do it."

"Only because he never in a million years dreamt we would."

"How about that?" A.E. grinned. She'd left instead of arguing with Sholto Douglas or warning him what she had in mind precisely so he wouldn't think to command her to keep her mouth shut.

Fleet Street had taken bomb damage. A.E. wondered if there was any part of London that hadn't. It was a big, big city, but the Germans had dropped a lot of explosives on it. The papers were very much in business despite everything. Some of the reporters were women, too, taking the place of men who'd put on one uniform or another. They seemed *most* interested in the story A.E. and Amy Johnson told.

"If I can get this past my editor, it'll make a head-line," one of them told A.E. "You may end up in hot water, though."

She shrugged. "Some Jerry may have shot me down by then, too. Next to that, what have I got to worry about? And all Amy's asking for is the chance to let the Germans shoot at her."

"Are all Americans barking mad?" the reporter asked.

"Nah." A.E. shook her head. "Just most of us."

Before she headed off to the train station from which she'd go back to Middle Wallop, she squeezed Amy. Anyone seeing them on the street would think they were two friends saying goodbye. Which they were, but ...

"Be careful," Amy said, and then, knowing that was foolish, "Be as careful as you can."

"I'd still be in Indiana if I did that. And now you're the one who wants to volunteer for the chance to get killed."

"It's my country, at least," Amy said.

"Right this minute, honey, it's everybody's country."

# CHAPTER ELEVEN

SHE FLEW AGAIN the next day. The Germans kept coming, though not in such numbers as before. The bomber pilots were getting leery; sometimes they'd order their loads of death dropped and scoot for France as soon as they saw RAF planes. Not all of them were such Aryan supermen that they didn't want to live.

When she landed after her second sortie, she found Flight Lieutenant Darley standing on the grass waiting for her. As soon as she climbed out of her Spit, he waved her over to him. "What have you done to get Marshal Douglas's knickers in a twist?" he demanded.

"Sir, I told him woman pilots like Amy Johnson might make better combat flyers than men without their training and experience."

"And how did he take that?"

"Not real well, sir."

"And did you just tell him this and then trot straight back here to Middle Wallop?"

A.E. hesitated. She hated to lie, but found herself tempted this time. In the end, she didn't. "No, sir. I told a few reporters the same thing."

Darley raised an eyebrow an eighth of an inch. An American officer would have been jumping up and down and screaming. The Englishman contented himself with murmuring, "You *do* like to live dangerously, don't you?"

"Sir, I'm flying a Spitfire. How many more chances can I take?"

"A point. Well, you're about to find out. You're ordered into London tomorrow. I wish you weren't. We're also going to lose our other three Yanks to 71 Squadron; the Eagles are finally going to fly together in squadron strength. I thought you'd be going along with them."

"So did I, sir." A.E. bit down hard on the inside of her lower lip. She'd got as close to Andy and Shorty and Red as you could in a few months' time. She wanted to stay with them. But she'd done what she'd done for Amy ... and now she might have to pay the price.

The Americans had a farewell bash that night. The men got snockered. A.E. didn't. She'd need her wits about her in the morning. Red said, "If Amy can fly the way you do, the Jerries better worry." Word got around fast—or maybe they'd seen some of the London papers. A.E. had by then. No wonder Sholto Douglas was annoyed at her. Some of them accused him of being next thing to a traitor.

She rode the train into the capital, then made her way to RAF HQ. This time, she didn't have to convince a sniffy flight lieutenant she deserved to see a senior officer. As soon as she gave her name, she was whisked up to Air Marshal Douglas's office, not quite under armed guard but not far from it.

When the aide who brought her in left, he closed the door behind him. Whatever Sholto Douglas had to say to her, he'd say it in privacy. He fixed her with a glare no doubt meant to put her in fear. She'd seen it done better. "Who gave you leave to blather to the newspapers?" he barked.

"No one, sir," A.E. said. "But nobody told me I couldn't, either."

"When you fly a mission, does your squadron commander order you not to shoot down the planes on your own side? You're assumed to have some small amount of sense on your own, you know."

A.E. stood mute.

When the air marshal realized she wasn't going to say anything, he clapped a dramatic hand to his forehead. Again, A.E. had seen better renditions. He went on, "Have you any notion how much trouble you've caused me these past two days? Any notion at all?"

"I was trying to help, sir," she said, which was true ... up to a point.

Douglas rolled his eyes. "God save us all if you take

it in your mind to harm! I've had reporters calling. I've had female-rights personages calling. I've had MPs calling, including that Robertson crackpot who's responsible for sneaking so many foreigners into the RAF."

He didn't say *so many stinking foreigners*, but his tone did the job for him. "Amy Johnson is as English as anyone, sir," A.E. replied. "She's a better pilot than almost anybody, too. Will you run her through OTU and let her help her country?"

"I've been ordered to do so, with her and certain other female pilots." Douglas spat out the words one by one, as if they tasted bad. He fixed her with another glare. "Which brings me to you. I have not been given any orders in your particular case, but allowed to use my own discretion."

"Sir." A.E. stood at attention—stood *to* attention, they said over here. No matter what he did, no matter how much it hurt, she was damned if she'd give him the satisfaction of showing anything.

"You are a bloody fool of a woman. You are a bloody fool of a Yank. You are bloody undisciplined and bloody insubordinate. And I am going to do the worst thing in the world I can think of to do to you."

"Sir," she repeated woodenly.

"I am not going to send you home and let you be a martyr. I am not going to waste time and effort court-martialing you. You've already cost the RAF far too much bad publicity. Oh, no! I'm going to do much worse than that."

"Sir?" A.E. said yet again. This time, though, she couldn't keep a bit of curiosity from her voice.

Sholto Douglas took what sounded like savage satisfaction in explaining, "I am ordering you to 71 Squadron. You bloody Yanks can have your bloody Eagle Squadron. Bound to be best any way one looks at it. At least we'll know all of you hooligans are in one place."

"Yes, sir." The air marshal would have known something was wrong had A.E. shrieked laughter in his face. Fool that he was, he'd given her exactly what she wanted. She wondered what he would have said if she'd come back with *Please don't throw me in the briar patch, sir!* It likely would have flown straight over his head. The Uncle Remus stories were much too American for the likes of him.

"Your transfer order and travel requisition will be waiting for you downstairs. Get the devil out of here," Douglas said.

A.E. saluted and left, still working not to laugh.

BY THE TIME she got to RAF Church Fenton, up in the West Riding of Yorkshire, she'd begun to believe Air Marshal Douglas really had done the worst thing he could to her. It was only 150 miles north of London, but it seemed like 1,500.

The train stopped at Selby, which was still several

miles away. Church Fenton was too small to boast a train station. A.E.'s uniform and ten shillings let her hire a bicycle to get her the rest of the way. She wondered whether a car had waited in Selby for Andy, Red, and Shorty.

Church Fenton, when she finally reached it, might have held a thousand people or might not. She had to ask directions to the air base. She barely understood the local dialect, though the people seemed to follow her well enough. They would have heard American accents in the movies, but broad Yorkshire was almost a foreign language to her.

At the air base, which lay northeast of the hamlet, she spotted Red Tobin at once. He was walking across bare grass; A.E. saw no airplanes. His face, which had been gloomy, lit up when he spied her pedaling his way. "What are you doing here?" he said.

She shrugged. "Air Marshal Douglas sent me here."

"Boy, he really must hate your guts."

"As a matter of fact, he does."

Red waved at the empty airstrip. "Here we are, the famous Eagle Squadron. Only thing is, where I come from the eagles have wings. Is it the same with you?"

"Now that you mention it, yes," A.E. said. "What are we supposed to be doing here, anyway?"

He got down on hands and knees and mimed cropping grass like a sheep. A.E. giggled. Red was always up for doing something crazy. As he bounced to his feet again, he pointed east. "The mouth of the Humber's that way, where it goes into the North Sea. Lots of shipping coming in and going out. Lots of shipping up and down the coast, too. We're here to drive off the Jerries if they make trouble. And if we ever get planes, of course."

"Of course," she echoed in a hollow voice. Here was Sholto Douglas's Eagle Squadron, chock full of Americans, stuck in the north end of nowhere to do nothing. "I wish they'd just left us where we were before."

"Believe you me, you ain't the only one. But c'mon into the barracks. Got something for you there, speaking of eagles." Red waved towards a Nissen hut not far away.

"You didn't even know I was coming." But A.E. followed him.

When he opened the door at the end, she saw Shorty and Andy playing cards with a couple of men she hadn't met before. "Look what the cat dragged in," Red said.

Her friends jumped up to shake her hand and clap her on the back. She got introduced to the others. They'd been scattered through the RAF before being gathered together here. Most of them seemed to have mixed feelings about the whole business, too. "I'd rather be doing something than doing nothing," one said.

The CO was an English flight lieutenant named Walter Churchill. The first thing he did was deny any relation to Winston. The next was to ask, "You knocked down a plane with 609 Squadron, is that right?"

"Two, sir," she replied.

"Jolly good. We can use you, sure enough," he said.

"Give her a patch!" Red said.

"One thing at a time, old man. One thing at a time." Churchill handed A.E. a round cloth patch a couple of inches across. It was of RAF dark blue, with a white eagle embroidered on it. The eagle held olive branches in one claw and arrows in the other, like the one on the Great Seal of the United States. Above its head and between its upraised wings were the letters ES.

Looking around, she saw that all the Eagles wore the patch near the top of their left sleeve. "Good to be one of the gang. Officially one of the gang," she said. Everybody whooped and clapped.

"Good to have you," Flight Lieutenant Churchill said. "The next question, now that you *are* one of the gang, is where shall we put you?"

"I slept in a tent at OTU and down at Middle Wallop," A.E. said, and thought of Amy. She wanted to blush. Instead, she went on, "That may not work so well, though, with the weather getting colder."

"No, likely not. If we give you a corner cot and rig blankets around it, will that do?" Churchill asked.

"I think so, sir. I hope so." A.E. wasn't about to say no. She knew her privacy wouldn't be perfect. She also knew the flyers were unlikely to be overwhelmed by whatever they saw. She was in good shape for her age, but her age was twice that of the barmaids and other women they were used to chasing.

"All right, then," Churchill said with a that's-settled smile.

But A.E. asked, "Sir, when will the squadron get some planes we can actually use?"

"We all want to know that," Shorty said.

Walter Churchill's smile disappeared. "I want to know that as much as anyone else. All I can tell you now is, I'm working on it." He sounded harassed. From her own brushes with RAF bureaucracy, A.E. could guess why.

# CHAPTER TWELVE

AS SUMMER GAVE way to autumn, days shortened fast. 71 Squadron continued to have everything it needed to become a functioning part of the RAF except planes. To say the Americans didn't take it well would have been one of the bigger understatements in the history of understatements. They drank. They gambled. Stacks of greenbacks and British banknotes changed hands at bridge, at poker, at craps. Then the winners drank some more to celebrate, the losers to drown their sorrows.

Americans didn't respect authority at the best of times. As week followed planeless week, the times got worse and worse. Walter Churchill was in something like genteel despair, trying to ride herd on men who had no use for him or anyone else connected to the RAF.

"I can talk to you," he said to A.E. one night when

the other Yanks were out carousing. "You've got more sense than they do. What am I supposed to do with them?"

"Look, I'm as fed up as they are. Only difference is, I don't think drinking myself blind is fun," she answered. "You want to solve everything in a hurry? Get us Spitfires, or even Hurricanes. Give us something worth doing."

He sent her an *Et tu, Brute?* look. "I'm trying. By God, I am. But we're stretched rather thin these days. You may possibly have noticed."

"You should have known better than to plop pilots down somewhere with nothing to fly—and nothing else to do, either."

"No doubt," Churchill said, and let it alone. He didn't confide in her again, not like that. If he'd wanted a shoulder to cry on, he hadn't got one.

She defended her fellow Yanks to the flight lieutenant, but she had trouble with them, too. She didn't like seeing Shorty, Andy, and Red as foul-mouthed and sodden as the rest of the Americans in the Eagle Squadron. But they at least knew her and respected her as a person and as a pilot. The others ...

She woke in the wee small hours one morning with weight pressing against the edge of the cot and a hand reaching under the blankets to grab her in places it had no business going. She wasn't surprised, even if she wished she would have been. She'd expected something of the sort for a couple of weeks now. She was ready if not eager.

Twisting away, she swung open-handed at where she guessed the groper's head would be. She made a good guess, and connected squarely. She didn't scream. Instead, she shouted as loud as she could, "Get out of here, you son of a bitch! Get away from me! What the hell do you think you're doing?"

All the snores and little nighttime noises in the Nissen hut cut off as if sliced by a knife. A startled, confused babble replaced them. In the blackness, someone beat a hasty, fumbling retreat.

Somebody's cot creaked as whoever it was hopped back into it. A.E. had an idea whose it was, but she wasn't sure. Part of her wanted to know, so she could either punch the bastard or swear out charges against him. Part of her insisted ignorance would be better. These kinds of problems were part of the reason fighting forces didn't want to let women join them.

She lay awake till the barracks roused at 0600. Then she looked to see whether anyone had a fresh mouse under one eye or a badly cleaned up bloody nose. She didn't see any evidence to make her grab someone and drag him up before the squadron. Maybe that was just as well. Maybe.

None of the American men said a word to her about what had happened during the night. *The dogs did nothing in the daylight,* she thought, mangling her Sherlock Holmes. That disappointed her but didn't much surprise her.

Even the thwarted assault didn't much surprise her. Like the powers that be, she'd known such things might happen, and she'd crossed the Atlantic anyhow. "Which makes me a fool or an optimist, one," she muttered under her breath, and headed to the mess hall for breakfast.

# CHAPTER THIRTEEN

A NEW LIAISON man joined the Eagles to give Walter Churchill a hand. Flying Officer Robbie Robertson was more than a bit of a toff. Some of the Yanks already seemed to know him, and he them. He was genial and quick with money when they ran dry. He seemed impossible to dislike, surely an asset for someone trying to keep some kind of rein on the American broncos.

And his name rang a bell with A.E., if only a vague one. She needed a couple of days before she figured out where she'd heard it. "You were an MP!" she blurted, adding, "Uh, sir"—he outranked her.

His smile, as usual, had charm to spare. "Well, yes, but it doesn't make me a bad person," he said. "Everyone agreed I'd do less damage in uniform than in the House of Commons, so here I am."

She didn't let his offhand manner deflect her. "You weren't just any old MP, though. You were the one who helped persuade the RAF to let me serve ... and other foreigners ... and Amy Johnson and those other women with her. Thank you, sir!"

"It wanted doing, so I did it," he said, and turned the subject.

A.E., by now, had got used to insistent English modesty. She didn't care for it—hiding your light under a bushel had never been an American virtue—but she'd come to grant it a certain reluctant respect. The people here who had most to brag about commonly bragged least. So she didn't push Robertson. Instead, she asked, "Can you do anything about getting us planes? I've heard fighter pilots do better with them."

His eyes twinkled. "Have you indeed? I confess, that same rumor's come to me."

"Well, then?"

"I'm doing whatever I can. Believe me, so is Flight Lieutenant Churchill. But 71 Squadron seems to lie well down the priority listing. I fear some Yanks' cowboy reputation doesn't improve matters. *Some* Yanks' reputation—present company very much excluded."

"Thanks," A.E. said dryly. Were you a cowboy if you stuck your hand between a fellow officer's legs? Were you a cowboy—or rather, a cowgirl—if you resented that and smacked the stupid, drunk, horny bastard, whoever he was? A.E. didn't care. As Robbie Robertson said, it wanted doing.

"Quite," he murmured, and then, "Do excuse me, please," which let him slip away. A.E. knew she wasn't the only American bending his ear about getting fighters. Andy called it banging on a teakettle when he didn't call it the same thing in Yiddish.

The Eagle Squadron's wings stayed clipped till the day after Halloween. Then, in its infinite wisdom and mercy, the RAF suffered seven Hurricane IIs to be delivered to Church Fenton. They were better than nothing. Not a great deal better than nothing, but enough. Spotting one would make a *Luftwaffe* bomber pilot think twice. A bastard in a 109, on the other hand ... You had a chance against the top German fighter in a Hurricane, but not a good chance.

Familiarizing herself with the Hurricane didn't take A.E. long. It reminded her of the Miles Master she'd flown at the OTU. She'd even heard a story that England had mounted half a dozen machine guns apiece on some Masters, to use them as emergency fighters and ground-attack planes if the Nazis invaded. She was damn glad it hadn't come to that; they lacked the performance to be anything but flying coffins.

A couple of days after the Hurricanes arrived, so did a letter from Amy. She'd passed fighter training and was posted to a squadron not far from Dover. She had a Spitfire, and gushed at its power. About her fellow pilots, she observed, *Well, we always did know men were rotters,* and let it go at that.

Remembering her own horrified awakening there in the darkness, A.E. could only nod. Amy closed the letter *Love and kisses,* which might mean anything or nothing.

One of these days, if they ever got leave at the same time, they might find out.

Meanwhile, the squadron moved south to Kirton Lindsey, outside of Scunthorpe. Kirton Lindsey was no duller than Church Fenton, but it wasn't much more exciting, either. The Eagles went to London whenever they could. They had a hard time buying their drinks, though they likely would have got just as smashed spending their own money.

Important people made much of them. "Quentin Reynolds wants to know what I think about how the war's going," Red Tobin told A.E. "Is that crazy or what?"

"That's crazy," she agreed. She knew she ought to go down to London herself and publicize the Eagle Squadron, but combat—with the Germans, with the RAF, and with her fellow Americans—had left her without the enthusiasm she needed to do a proper job.

Andy Mamedoff caught the eye of a cigarette manu-facturer's daughter named Penny Craven. "Her family's got stacks—I mean, stacks," he reported. "She knows I'm broke, but she thinks I'm wonderful anyway."

"Good for you," A.E. said. She wouldn't have if he hadn't seemed smitten himself, but he did. The only thing about love she was sure of was that she wasn't sure of anything about love. Some people did make it work, though. Maybe Andy and Penny would.

Or maybe they wouldn't get the chance to. 71 Squadron was flying patrols over the North Sea now. It was hard, demanding, dangerous work. German 109s weren't the problem; they were still far enough north to be out of range of *Luftwaffe* fighters. But flying over the cold gray sea in weather that kept getting worse took everything a pilot had. Some didn't have enough.

A.E. mourned with the other Eagles when somebody didn't make it back to the airstrip, though she didn't get savagely drunk at wakes the way they did. But the memory of a hand in the dark kept her from being as sorrowful as she might have been otherwise.

As 1940 passed into 1941, she got another letter from Amy. Still down near the south coast, the English flyer was scooting across the Channel to shoot up German installations in France. *It's mad fun,* she wrote. *They did it to us. Now we get to pay them back. I hope they like it even less than we did.*

A.E. wanted to be doing something like that, wanted it enough to taste it. She understood the need for the job she was doing. She understood better by the day the exacting care it took to fly mission after mission and come back safe to base every time. Not everyone could do it. The wakes they'd held proved that. Bad luck, a dumb mistake, a breakdown ...

But she'd never felt more alive than in those September days when she battled the *Luftwaffe* high above burning London. What was that Cole Porter line? *I get no kick from champagne / Mere alcohol doesn't thrill me at all*—that was it. She'd got a kick from machine guns, though, and another one because the Germans had machine guns and cannon of their own.

Amy sounded as if she was getting the same kick now, taking the air war to the Nazis. Well, she deserved it. She'd been green with envy that night at Middle Wallop, that night when mad things happened. And she was fighting to defend her own homeland, not borrowing someone else's cause.

"Good for her," A.E. murmured, and then, "Lord, I hope she makes it." It was as close to a prayer as she'd come in many years. She had a small box with a lock. A hammer could smash it open, but it was the best she could do. She tucked the letter in there and locked it away from the world.

# CHAPTER FOURTEEN

JUST INTO THE NEW YEAR, Walter Churchill got promoted to wing commander and sent to a new post. A Yank, an ex-Navy man turned RAF flight leader named William Taylor, took over for him. 71 Squadron was all-American at last. Taylor was a much tougher disciplinarian than Churchill had been, so not all the Eagles were thrilled with the change.

They lost a pilot in early February. Combat had nothing to do with it. He made a mistake flying low and hit the ground before he could correct it. Back in the States, the news would make winter even colder for his family.

A week later, a section from 71 Squadron scrambled in response to something out on the North Sea. It wasn't A.E.'s section, so she didn't worry about what it was. They'd do whatever needed doing or they'd find out it was a false alarm, then they'd fly back.

Only one of them didn't. Shorty Keough wasn't at the mess table that night.

"He and another guy dove into a cloudbank," one of the other pilots said glumly. "I don't think he pulled out of it. Straight into the drink, fast as a Hurricane can go. He never knew what hit him, that's for goddamn sure."

A.E. didn't know what had hit her. She and Shorty had been part of this mad venture together since the very first day, in the hotel at Montreal. Andy and Red looked poleaxed, too. You didn't want to believe, you couldn't make yourself believe, it could happen to somebody with whom you'd been through so much.

Robert Ripley's words tolled in her head like the mourning bell in a church steeple. Believe It or Not.

Shorty'd made people notice him. There wasn't much of him, but what there was was full of life. Nobody wanted to think he'd died so pointlessly. But then the Coast Guard found wreckage off the coast. Floating on the cold, merciless sea were, among other things, a pair of size five flying boots. Shorty might have been the only pilot in the RAF to wear boots so small. No doubt could be left.

Everyone got very drunk, A.E. with the rest of the Eagles. Red and Andy, in particular, were stunned the same way she was. "He could have been my brother," Red kept saying over and over.

"Life's a bastard," Andy said. "You go up in a crate, you have to pray everything works just the way it's supposed to. If it doesn't, you ain't coming back."

"Life's a bastard," A.E. said. "Leave it right there."

"Yeah." Mamedoff shook his head. "Shorty and his stupid cushions. You'd see him in the cockpit with just the top of his head poking up and you'd want to bust a gut laughing, but he could fly."

"He could fly," A.E. agreed. That was the best epitaph Shorty Keough was likely to get. She admired Andy for summing him up so perfectly in three words. She put an arm around him about the same time he put an arm around her.

"I'm gonna go outside and have a cigarette," he said, though the air in the officers' mess was blue with smoke. "Wanna come out with me and we can talk for a little bit?"

"Sure," she said.

It was chilly out there, and damp with the threat of rain. In the blackout, the brief flare of his match seemed like a flashbulb. He took two fierce drags on the Woodbine, then threw it down and stepped on it. "Ah, hell," he said. "Nothing's any goddamn good anymore."

"I know," A.E. said softly.

He reached for her then. She squeezed him back. They were about the same height; they fit together well. His mouth tasted of whiskey and tobacco. When they separated, he whispered, "Let's find somewhere."

"What about Penny?"

"What about her? She doesn't know Shorty. She's met him, but she doesn't *know* him. She doesn't know about any of ... this. She's lucky."

A.E. understood exactly what he meant. She slipped away from the Nissen hut with him. It was more a catharsis than a rapture, but catharsis was what they both needed. Afterwards, she said, "You're squashing me."

"Sorry," he replied, and took his weight on knees and elbows. He started putting himself back together with what seemed to A.E. like practiced ease. A little more slowly, she followed suit. He said, "Maybe we should go on to the barracks instead of back to the bash. Then nobody'll be able to pin anything on us for sure."

"Good idea," she said, running fingers through her hair to make sure she had no leaves stuck in it. She added, "I bet Shorty's laughing, wherever he is."

"Funny—I was thinking the same thing." Andy hesitated, then said, "You're all right, you know? Not 'cause you're famous or anything, I mean. Because you're you."

"Thanks." A.E. wondered if she'd ever heard anything she was more grateful for. Her fame was a big part of what had driven George to her; she'd understood that right from the start. Its starting to slip was a big part of why he'd lost interest, too. Being valued for who she was, not what she was, made her happy in a way very different from Andy's gentle roughness moments before.

She let him lead the way to the barracks, and went in a couple of minutes after he did. She found her cot and fell asleep with a smile on her face.

# CHAPTER FIFTEEN

SHE WAS STILL SMILING when she woke the next
morning, but not for long. Two worries darkened her
thoughts like storm clouds. The first took care of itself a
few days later, when her period came. Getting pregnant
at forty-three wasn't likely, but ... Her mind's eye had
been seeing headlines like KNOCKED-UP PILOT
DRUMMED OUT OF RAF!

The second was that Andy Mamedoff might make
trouble if she turned him down when he tried his luck
again. But he didn't try again. As far as she could judge
from the way he acted, what had happened might as well
not have. Maybe it had been just another way to mourn
Shorty. Maybe he didn't want to take any chances with
landing Penny Craven. Or maybe he hadn't thought she
was such hot stuff.

Whatever the reason, he stayed as he'd been since
the day they met: cocky, amused and amusing, ironically

detached. He didn't let on that anything out of the ordinary had happened, and neither did she.

She did try to get some leave so she could go south to visit Amy. When she managed it, she sent a wire saying she'd take the train down the following Tuesday.

Monday night, she was throwing things into a little suitcase when an answering telegram came back. She opened the envelope and read the message on the flimsy yellow paper. REGRET TO INFORM YOU PILOT OFFICER JOHNSON MISSING, PRESUMED LOST, OVER FRANCE. PLANE SEEN ON FIRE, NO CHUTE. Amy Johnson's squadron leader's printed signature followed.

A.E. stared at the message for two or three minutes. It wasn't that she didn't understand it; more that she didn't want to understand it. She'd pushed Amy toward flying in combat, pushed her harder than she'd felt comfortable going herself. Amy'd got to do it, and she'd paid the full price for being treated like a man.

Maybe she would have wanted that. Maybe she would have been happier ferrying planes around the British Isles till the war finally ended, if it ever did. She wouldn't get to make a choice like that now, though. The most A.E. could hope for was that she'd done some more damage before she bought her plot.

Dully, she got to her feet. Flight Lieutenant Taylor was doing paperwork when he probably should have been grabbing what shuteye he could. A.E. stood in front of the beat-up card table he used for a desk and waited to be noticed. In due course, he looked up. "Yes, Pilot Officer?"

"Sir, I ... I won't need that leave I asked for after all." A.E. could hear her own voice shake.

Bill Taylor raised an eyebrow. "'Won't need leave'? What kind of language is that?"

All A.E. could do was hold out the telegram. "This is Amy Johnson, sir. The pilot. My friend. We'd known each other for years. I was going down to see her. Not much point now, is there?"

"Amy Johnson? Good God! Yes, of course you'd know each other, wouldn't you? I'm sorry!" Taylor paused in visible thought. "Don't you want leave anyway? You could go somewhere and think about something that's got nothing to do with flying till you come back."

"But flying's the only thing I care about, sir," A.E. said. "The only people in England who matter to me now—the only ones who're still alive, I mean—are right here."

"We're a band of brothers," Taylor said slowly. "You've shown a band of brothers can have room in it for a sister as well. And so did Pilot Officer Johnson, no doubt about it."

It seemed to A.E. that he gave Amy due respect by using her rank rather than her name. You were born male or female. Rank, you had to earn. *Whether the bastards want you to or not,* she thought. Managing a salute, she said, "Thank you very much, sir," and let him get back to it.

The next morning, she was helping the mechanics work on the Hurricane she flew. The better you took care of your kite, the better it would take care of you. She was greasy to the elbows, with her mind on engine valves and nothing else, when Red Tobin said, "I thought you got yourself leave. God knows you could use some. You stay here more than anybody else, and this isn't exactly bright lights and big city."

That, of course, brought everything flooding back. But Red was as much a friend as Andy, even if they hadn't lain down together. He was as much a friend as she had over here now that Shorty and Amy were gone. She told him about the wire she'd got.

He kicked at the grass under his boots. "*Ahhhh,* hell," he said. "That's about as rotten as it gets. If anybody was gonna speak your lingo, she'd be the one."

"Yes!" she said, glad he understood, well, most of what she was feeling and also wondering if she was that easy to read for people who didn't know her so well.

"You need a shoulder to cry on, I'm around." He didn't push it any further than that, but ambled away. In his easygoing, offhand style, he was a gentleman. She wondered why she'd taken so long to notice.

Shrugging, she leaned back into the Hurricane's engine compartment and started guddling around in its guts once more. Work brought forgetfulness, or at least it might.

IN APRIL, 71 Squadron moved down to Martlesham Heath in Suffolk. There were bogies there. They chased German bombers and tangled with 109s. Every time A.E. saw one of those small, squared-off fighters, she wondered if the pilot was the one who'd bounced Amy. That she knew she'd never find out didn't stop the wondering.

The Eagles moved again in July, to North Weald, just outside of London. They graduated back to Spitfires, too—Spitfire Vs, with two cannon and four machine guns.

"Now we're in next week, not last week," Red Tobin said.

"About time, too," Andy added.

With the better planes, they'd soon start raiding France themselves. Everyone said so, anyhow. The RAF called the cross-Channel shoot-'em-ups Rhubarbs. To A.E., that brought to mind brawls on a baseball diamond. Her fellow pilots laughed, though no one from England would have thought it was funny.

A couple of Yanks left 71 Squadron to join 121 Squadron, the second outfit full of Eagles. She thought one of them was the man who'd groped her in the Nissen hut in the middle of the night, but she couldn't prove it. When they threw him his farewell bash, she made sure she stayed sober.

By the time 71 Squadron did start making Rhubarb

raids, fewer German planes were left in France to fight them. Hitler had jumped on Stalin, and he threw all he could into the big fight in the east. It was as if he meant to deal with England later, once Russia was down for the count.

A.E. didn't care much. The chance to go after the Nazis and hurt them in land they held felt irresistible to her. They'd caused England so much misery. If they couldn't keep the RAF from getting some of its own back now, too bad for them.

The squadron leader understood what his pilots were feeling. All the same, he told them, "Don't make like a hero unless that's your only choice. Heroes have a bad habit of not coming back, and we need you to fly more missions against the Jerries. Chances are, they won't come up against you. If they do, we'll spot them on radar and warn you by radio. Don't let them cut you off from England. Steer around them if you can and come home. Have you got that, you goddamn thick-skulls?"

None of the pilots told him no. A.E. wondered how seriously they took his words, though. She wondered how seriously she took them herself. All the same, she couldn't help remembering what she'd heard when she first came to 609 Squadron. *Most of the men sitting here with you will be dead a year from now.* That came much too close to prophecy straight out of the Old Testament.

She flew her first Rhubarb with Red Tobin a few days later. He flew as leader, she as his wingman. Another

English pair crossed the Channel with them. Bit by bit, the RAF was abandoning three-plane vics and squadrons in rigid formation. The *Luftwaffe* grouping they called the finger-four—two pairs of leaders and wingmen, all watching out for one another—had proved a lot more flexible.

They zoomed over the Channel in nothing flat. She'd taken much longer to fly that, *ah*, borrowed Potez from south to north. A year ago now. How was that possible? The only thing that made her believe it was how much she'd learned about the pilot's art since. Flying the Atlantic, even flying around the world, couldn't touch combat for teaching you what you needed to know. They couldn't touch it for killing you off if you didn't learn, either.

France. The raiders went in low, just over a thousand feet. Normandy looked like England. The roads were even emptier, though. The only motorized vehicles on them would belong to the Germans.

Hardly had that crossed A.E.'s mind than she spied four trucks chugging down a country road, all in a line. Next to American Studebakers or Fords, they weren't big trucks, but they'd have Nazis in them. She pushed the stick forward and stooped on them like a falcon taking field mice.

Her thumb stabbed the red firing button. A Spitfire's aerodynamics were so good, you hardly felt the recoil when you opened up. Bits and pieces flew from the trucks as bullets and shells slammed home. Men bailed out and ran for the roadside hedges. One of the trucks caught fire.

A.E. felt no guilty twinge as she pulled up. One more lesson combat had taught her was that the other guys would kill you if you gave them even a quarter of a chance. The best way to stay alive if you were going to fight at all was to hurt them as much as you could. Some Germans wouldn't have got out of the trucks. Some might be burning up now.

*Yes? And so?* she thought. They'd done worse to England the year before. They still sent raiders over whenever they could. This was what war was all about.

By the radio chatter in her earphones, the other pilots had also found ways to annoy the Jerries. Red's voice sounded confident as he said, "Let's make for the meet-up point and head on home."

She acknowledged. So did the men in the other pair. The meet-up point was Goury lighthouse, not far west of Cherbourg. As long as nobody in the *Luftwaffe* knew that, they were fine.

Meet up there they did, and then head north across the sea. Even in summer, the water looked cold. A.E. thought of Shorty Keough, and wished she hadn't.

After they landed, Red said, "There better be rhubarb pie for dessert tonight, or I'll know the reason why."

"Rhubarb pie?" A.E. didn't care for it. Then the joke got home. She rolled her eyes. "You're impossible, Red!"

Tobin saluted extravagantly. "No, ma'am, just

improbable." They both laughed. Sometimes you could, even in the middle of a war. Sometimes, by God, you had to.

JULY SLID INTO AUGUST. Andy Mamedoff got promoted to flying officer, the first American fighter jockey to rise a grade. He was going to 133 Squadron, a third outfit full of Yanks, and the plan was for him to lead one of the flights in the new Eagle Squadron.

When A.E. congratulated him on coming up in the world, he made a face. "Ah, cut the crap, willya?" he said. "We all know it shoulda been you. You're the best pilot here, and it ain't close. It woulda been you, I bet, if only—" He didn't go on, or need to.

She shrugged. "I can do without the aggravation. You'll just have to give orders. I'd need to convince another bunch of wild men from Borneo I knew what I was doing before they'd decide maybe they should take me seriously."

"It shouldn't work that way," Andy said.

"I know. But it does." And she would have had the advantage of fame working for her. So would poor Amy if she'd lived long enough to win promotion. It would have been four times as hard for an ordinary woman who also just happened to be a superior officer.

Even with the advantage of fame, that goddamn French doctor had felt her up. And one of her fellow

American pilots had embarked on what would have been a rape if she'd been scared into silence the way he no doubt hoped. A man wouldn't have had to worry about that kind of crap, either.

*One thing at a time,* she told herself. *First we whip Hitler. Then we start putting our own house in order. We sure as hell need to.*

# CHAPTER SIXTEEN

ANDY'S WEDDING to Penny Craven was in Epping, the next town west of North Weald. The bride looked smashing. Andy looked like a cat about to start licking cream from a pitcher his people had forgotten about.

After the ceremony, A.E. lined up outside the church with other flyers from the original Eagle Squadron. As the new bride and groom walked between their short rows, Mamedoff tipped her a wink. He turned his head to make sure his new wife didn't see him doing it, too. A.E. grinned. She had all she could do not to laugh out loud. He was a piece of work, all right.

The reception was on the meadow behind the home —the mansion, really—of Penny's father and mother. "So wonderful to meet you, Pilot Officer Earhart," Penny said. "I've admired you since I was a child, of course. And Andy always says such wonderful things about you."

"Does he?" A.E. kept her face straight. As far as she was concerned, that came closer to earning her a medal than anything she'd done in the air against the Germans.

Before the new Mrs. Mamedoff could answer, two Spitfires from 71 Squadron buzzed the reception. They weren't much above rooftop height, and did a victory roll as they passed overhead. The roar from their motors stopped everything in its tracks. A.E. glanced at the big house's windows to make sure they hadn't shivered to sparkling shards.

"The cheek of those buggers!" someone said when mere human conversation became possible again. "I shall speak to the RAF about this."

"You do that, sir," someone else told him. Before long, A.E. realized the man who'd complained was Epping's mayor. Maybe the flyers really would wind up in trouble.

She glanced back to Penny. All the Englishwoman said was, "Do you Yanks do that every time somebody in the squadron gets married?"

"I don't know," A.E. answered. "Andy's the first one."

Penny Craven—no, Penny Mamedoff now—smiled a smile of ownership. A.E. could have told her something about that, but she didn't. She wanted Andy to be happy. God only knew he'd earned happiness the hard way. She did wonder if Penny knew Andy's folks ran a restaurant in Massachusetts. She wondered even more if Penny's father and mother knew. That smile said the new bride was marrying for love, or thought she was. She might not worry so much about money. Her parents would, though.

"Americans certainly have livened things up since they got here," Penny said. "We can use some of that, I think."

"I'm not the one to tell you whether you can use it or not," A.E. said. "But you're right. You've sure got it."

AFTER A SEVERELY ABBREVIATED WARTIME HONEYMOON, Andy went off to his new squadron. A.E. caught Red Tobin sending her quizzical looks. "What's up?" she asked, as usual not beating around the bush.

"I dunno," he said. But even he could tell that wouldn't do. He tried again: "Ain't nobody left here but us chickens."

"Don't say it like that!" she exclaimed.

"Sorry," he answered sheepishly. "You know what I mean, though."

"I know how you said it—like we'll be gone pretty soon, too. Cut that out, you hear?" If A.E. hadn't had any superstitions like that before, flying in wartime would have given them to her. Too many strange things and too many horrible things happened for you just to shrug them off. She didn't like thinking she heard the goose walking over her grave.

A few days later, Red said, "We've got another Rhubarb set for tomorrow. You coming with me again?"

"If I can," she said. "When I was flying patrol over the Channel just now, my engine started smoking and trying to cut out. I had to nurse it back here at low power. After I landed, I checked it, but I couldn't find anything. The mechanics are trying to figure out what's wrong with it now."

"Okay. You sure as heck don't want to go over France in a kite that might let you down. I'll talk to one of the guy guys"—he grinned at her—"in case you can't make it."

He flew with a different wingman the next day. The groundcrew still hadn't made her Spitfire's Merlin behave. A.E. felt bad about staying behind, but what could you do? No one would question her courage; she'd done more than enough to prove that to the other flyers even if she was a woman. But she *wanted* to cross the Channel and kick the Germans in the teeth, dammit.

Eight planes did climb away from North Weald: two finger-fours. They had enough firepower among them to hit the enemy hard if they came across anything juicy. A.E. watched them fly south and wished them luck. She'd see them all again—she hoped she'd see them all again—in two or three hours. She wondered what kind of stories they'd tell.

She realized something had gone wrong well before the Rhubarb raiders were due back. A corporal on a bicycle came from the radar station to the operations hut as fast as he could pedal. He didn't waste time on the kickstand when he got there. The bike fell over with a clatter as he dashed inside.

When he came out, his face was still as white as if he'd seen a ghost. A.E. dogtrotted over to him as he picked up the bicycle. "What happened?" she said. "Something must have."

"Aye, ma'am." He nodded jerkily. He had a northern accent. A.E. had been in England long enough by now to recognize it. "There's Jerries oop behind t'boys, swarms o' Jerries. They laid a trap, like, an' we walked into it."

"Christ! Can our guys get away?"

"Soon as we saw 'em go oop, I came over here. T'boys know they've got trouble now. They'll do what they can." The corporal lit a cigarette and offered A.E. the packet. She shook her head. He rode back to the radar station.

And she ... was all dressed up with no place to go. She looked toward her kite, and toward the mechanics still working on it. She could have been down in France herself, goddammit. She might have done Red some good.

More of the RAF men who stayed on the ground all the time started gathering at the edge of the runway with extinguishers and other firefighting gear. The shoulder-length asbestos gauntlets made A.E. suck in her breath. If you had to wear those to pull someone from a burning plane, would he thank you for it afterwards?

Four planes came back, all of them colandered with bullet holes, two with wounded pilots. "God bless the fucking planes," one Yank said, sounding more than half drunk on adrenaline and terror. "They can give it out, and Jesus, they can take it. We all oughta be dead."

"What happened ... to the guys who aren't here?" A.E. asked.

"They went down. If they're lucky, they got out first. If they're real lucky, they'll run into friendly Frenchmen and get fed toward Spain and Portugal, and maybe we'll see 'em again. Otherwise, POW camps. Or ..." He didn't go on, or need to.

Red Tobin wasn't one of the Americans who'd returned. No one had seen him bail out. A.E. stumbled around the base in a mixture of grief and guilt. When he would have needed her most, she was stuck on the wrong side of the Channel.

What could you do now? You could get drunk, and A.E. did. Booze put a glass wall between what you were feeling and you. It didn't go away, but you got some shelter from it. You could screw. You forgot everything else when you did, at least for a little while. If Andy'd been around, A.E. might have, and what Penny didn't find out about wouldn't hurt her. But none of the other Yanks in 71 Squadron interested her that way. At least nobody tried to jump on her after she fell into her cot.

The next morning, her head pounded as if she had a drop forge in there. Aspirins and coffee helped as much as they could: better than nothing, but not good enough.

She went out to see how the mechanics were doing with her Spit.

"We've set it right, ma'am," the flight sergeant in charge of the work crew told her. He smiled. "Good job we didn't fix it yesterday, what? You might've got caught in France yourself."

He meant well. She reminded herself of that before she could start shrieking obscenities at him. All the same, her stare made him flinch. "I wanted to be there," she said in a low, deadly voice. "One of the two best friends I had left on this side of the ocean got killed yesterday. Maybe I could have done something to keep him alive."

"I'm very sorry, ma'am," the mechanic said, and got away from her as fast as he could. She didn't suppose she could blame him.

# CHAPTER SEVENTEEN

WHAT SHE'D HEARD in 609 and 71 Squadrons was true: oxygen did more for a hangover than anything else. She took the Spitfire out over the Channel on patrol, fiercely hoping to meet a German plane. Red deserved revenge. Who better to give it to him than she?

No Ju 88s or He 111s high up. No low-flying 109s trying a reverse Rhubarb, perhaps with a medium-sized bomb slung under the fuselage as an extra present for England. A few freighters crawled along down below, hugging the coastline like a life jacket. With most of the *Luftwaffe* tied up in Russia, the Jerries didn't hit shipping the way they had the year before.

The year before ... *I'm still here,* A.E. thought. *Andy is, too. But how many are left from 609 Squadron now?* To her shame, she wasn't sure. She'd fallen out of touch with her old outfit after transferring to the Eagles. That was part of war, too. The past stopped counting. Only what you were doing right now meant anything. Tomorrow? Time to worry about tomorrow if you were still here then.

She flew through her assigned area. Seeing nothing out of the ordinary, she reported the nothing: one more blank piece on the puzzlemap of England and its surrounding waters. She hoped the rest of the country-wide map was just as untroubled.

When her fuel began running low, she swung the Spitfire back toward North Weald. Her landing was as uneventful as the rest of the patrol. Another day's duty done. Another day like most days—except Red Tobin was dead; he wouldn't make any more silly jokes, and back in Los Angeles his folks and his girlfriend would be getting the news they dreaded most.

They'd have to find a way to go on without him, the same as A.E. would. She knew he wrote to them all the time. Maybe that would help keep him alive in their hearts, or maybe looking at his letters would hurt too much to bear. They'd work it out one way or another. So would A.E.

If you weren't going to go crazy, you had to. People, even people you cared about, people you loved, were around for only so long. If you happened to be left behind after they went, well, wherever they went, you mourned and you let time blunt the hurt and heal the wound and you went on. And when you stopped going on, other people would mourn you till time blunted that hurt, too. Life worked like that. It struck A.E. as a rotten game, but it was the one the world had.

She flew her patrols and reported her nothing back by radio till one day, a couple of weeks after Red didn't come back from France, she reported something instead. A bomber was flying across the Channel, heading for England. It wasn't far above the waves. If it came in low, English radar had a harder time spotting it.

This time, though, the good old Mark One eyeball had spotted it. "Am attacking," A.E. said, and heeled her Hurricane over into a dive. It was a Ju 88, she saw, the best model the Germans used. It was both faster and better armed than the Do 17 or the He 111. Against a fighter, though, especially a fighter with the altitude edge, none of that was likely to do it much good.

The gunner at the rear of the cockpit opened up on her at the same time as the pilot started jinking frantically. As with the 110 that had been her first kill, one machine gun wasn't enough defensive firepower. A few tracers flew close enough to make her want to duck, but she poured 20mm and machine-gun rounds into the starboard wing till smoke billowed from the engine and flames licked toward the fuselage.

She pulled back on the stick and did a long loop to set herself up for another run at the bomber. As soon as she got far enough around, she saw she wouldn't need it. The Junkers had gone into the drink. How many men did it carry? Five, she thought. Well, they were five who wouldn't give England any more trouble.

"Target destroyed," she reported, remembering the radio. Easier to call it that. Then you didn't have to think of the men inside at all.

"Well done!" came the reply. It was done, all right, well or otherwise.

When she landed back at North Weald—a bit earlier than she'd planned, since the full-power attack run used more fuel than routine flight—the squadron leader stood out on the grass to greet her. "I hear you got a bomber," Flight Lieutenant Taylor said.

"Yes, sir."

"How many is that for you now?"

"Three, sir."

"You'll make ace before you know it."

"I'm still around, sir. That's a big part of it right there."

"You're right." Bill Taylor nodded vigorously. "You're green as paint the first few times you go into action. Baptism by total immersion, nothing else but. If you last long enough to see what you need to do—grow your eyes on swivel stalks, mostly—you start to have a chance up there."

"That's about the size of it," A.E. agreed. But part of it was luck, too. If some of the Ju 88's machine-gun bullets had slammed into her engine, she would have gone into the Channel instead of the Germans. As at Monte Carlo, the odds were sure to bite you if you played long enough. Sooner or later, you'd roll snake eyes and crap out. You hoped for later. Hope was all you could do.

"How are you going to celebrate this one?" he asked.

She stared at him. "I hadn't even thought about it. Can I have a couple of extra hours of sack time tomorrow morning?"

"You got 'em. I wish everybody was so easy to please. But you don't go out and tie one on like the guys, do you?"

"Not ... very often," A.E. said. "I'm more likely to do it on account of something bad. After Red didn't come back, and Shorty before him ..."

"I understand. Well, good job today, that's for sure." Taylor gave her a brisk nod. She saluted. He turned and went off to do whatever he needed to do next.

The other pilots in the Eagle Squadron congratu-lated her through the afternoon and at dinner. They teased her for not wanting to go out and get drunk, but they didn't push her too hard. They'd got used to her ways, and to having her in the squadron. Maybe, now, they wouldn't try to jump on her if they got pickled enough and horny enough. Or maybe they would anyhow. You never could tell.

They did do their best to stay quiet in the morning so she could enjoy her extra sleep. Since she hadn't expected them to care even that much, she was delighted. Then life got back to normal.

IT STOPPED BEING normal again on a chilly, cloudy day in early October, when she was glad she could find her way back to North Weald from her patrol flight and even gladder the clouds didn't go all the way down to the deck. She landed inartistically, but not enough so as to damage her Spitfire. As soon as she saw the groundcrew men's faces, she knew something was wrong.

She opened the cockpit and said, "For God's sake, what is it?" even before undoing her harness and getting out.

They all looked at one another, which only frightened her more. At last, the senior man, a sergeant, licked his lips and said, "We got the word, ma'am, just after you took off. I'm sorry, ma'am."

"Got the word of *what*? Sorry for *what*?" She didn't like hearing her voice rise that way, but she couldn't help it.

"That's right—she don't know," one mechanic said to another in a low voice.

The crew chief licked his lips again. "Ma'am, last night Pilot Officer Mamedoff—no, Flying Officer Mamedoff, 'e was now—'e was taking a flight to a field on the Isle of Man. There was fog, worse there than it 'as been 'ere, and ..." The words that mattered came out in a rush: "'E flew into the side of a hill, ma'am, and three more planes with 'im. They all died. It was over in a hurry, anyway."

"Andy? No," she whispered. Andy'd been smart. He'd been sensible. He must not have been smart or sensible enough, though. With agonizing clarity, she remembered how they'd consoled each other after Shorty bought a plot. She had no one left with whom she wanted to do anything like that now. And it was nothing she could talk about with anyone else. Instead, she said, "My God, his poor wife! Penny must be frantic. They only just got married!"

"Yes, ma'am," the sergeant said. "Flight Lieutenant Taylor, 'e's over there in Epping now, to break the news."

That was a job A.E. wouldn't have wanted for all the money in the world. Having to write letters of condolence was bad enough. To go tell a gorgeous young newlywed that she was suddenly a widow, to do it in person ...

"It's a rum go, ma'am," the sergeant offered. "A rum go all around."

"Yes. It is." A.E. heard her own voice as if from very far away. She climbed out of the cockpit and hopped down from the wing to the grass. She had no idea what her face looked like. Whatever it was, it made the groundcrew men part before her like the Red Sea before Moses.

Maybe she looked like death itself. She wouldn't have been surprised. She'd seen too much of it, this past year and more. In the Spanish Civil war, there'd been a Fascist general who led his troops into battle with the cry *¡Viva la muerte!*—Long live death! Back in the States,

she'd thought him an utter savage when she heard that.
Now ...

Now she just didn't know. War was about killing
people on the other side till the ones left alive did what
you told them to. She'd come to Europe, come to
England, to kill Germans. She'd damn well done it, too.
And now none of the friends who'd come over with her
was still alive himself.

You could drink yourself into oblivion every chance
you got. You could screw like there was no tomorrow.
Very often, there wasn't. So much of war involved hiding
from the grinning skull that lurked behind all the patri-
otic posters and songs and movies and slogans. War
meant death. Everything else about it just covered
that up.

She stumbled into the barracks. Some of the pilots
were sitting and kneeling on the floor, redistributing
wealth with a pair of dice. They looked up when she
came in. Seeing her face, one of them said, "Guess you
heard."

"Yeah." She managed a nod. Even to her, it seemed
to have come from a mechanism that desperately needed
oiling.

She pushed past the blankets that walled off her cot
from the rest, lay down, and stared at the corrugated
galvanized iron of the arched ceiling. No answers there.
No answers anywhere. All you could do was go on.
Sooner or later, something would stop you from even
that.

She closed her eyes. What she saw on the insides of her eyelids was worse than corrugated galvanized iron, so she opened them again. The guys shooting craps were quieter than usual, perhaps out of sympathy.

After a while, someone else walked in. She thought she recognized Bill Taylor's stride even before he said, "I saw Earhart's kite on the field. Is she here?"

"Yes, sir," one of the men answered. She heard him shift; he might have been pointing toward her corner spot.

Taylor came that way. Outside the blankets, he asked, "Can I come in?"

"Yes, sir." A.E. sat up.

When the squadron CO did, his face told her something about what hers had to look like. "Bastardly news," he said. "I mean, bastardly."

"Yes, sir," she repeated.

"I'm just back from Epping, and ..." He didn't go on.

"They told me you were there. I'm sorry you had to do that. I'm sorry about ... about everything right now."

"So is everybody who knew Andy. It's a miserable business, that's all. The past couple of hours ..." Taylor shook himself like a dog coming out of cold water. "I think I'd rather have the Jerries shoot me down than go through that again."

"I believe it. At least when the Jerries get you, it's done fast," A.E. said. It had ended fast for Andy. He'd never known what hit him—or rather, what he'd hit.

That small mercy stood out in a world conspicuously lacking larger ones.

"Take care of yourself. We have to stay in the game any which way we can." The squadron CO slid out of the blanket-walled cubicle.

# CHAPTER EIGHTEEN

THE FUNERAL WAS as bad as she'd expected. They buried Andy in a closed coffin, which meant the undertaker hadn't been able to make him presentable. Behind black veiling, Penny Mamedoff looked shattered. A.E. wondered what Andy would think of spending eternity in an Anglican churchyard. Since he'd happily got married in an Anglican church, chances were he wouldn't mind.

Along with the Office for the Dead, the minister read a sonnet called "High Flight."

"The author, Pilot Officer John Gillespie Magee, Jr., is one of Flying Officer Mamedoff's fellow Eagles," he said. A.E. had seen the poem before; it got widely printed in papers and magazines. She didn't think Pilot Officer Magee would put Shakespeare on the bread line any time soon, but she appreciated the sentiment.

AND THE WAR GROUND ON. As weather wors-
ened, flying time went down. On one patrol, she spotted
a 109 with a bomb slung under its belly. But its pilot
spied her, too. He dumped the bomb in the Channel and
got the hell out of there. She decided to count herself
lucky. If he'd decided to fight it out, an unencumbered
109 was a match for a Spitfire.

She was going in to dinner on a cold Sunday evening
when another pilot came running up behind her shouting, "Holy jumping Jesus, the Japs have bombed Pearl
Harbor—I just heard it on the radio!"

"Oh, my God!" somebody else exclaimed. "The
USA's finally in the war for real!"

All through the meal, the men gabbled excitedly
about how the Eagle Squadrons were bound to get
folded into the US Army Air Force sooner than soon.
A.E. ate without trying to argue with them.

For one thing, though Japan had attacked the United
States, Germany hadn't, not really. Could FDR get
Congress to declare war on the Nazis anyway? For
another ... If the States did get into the European war,
she thought the Eagles had it straight. The USA would
incorporate them into its forces. Them, yes. But her?
England had been desperate, fearing the first successful
invasion since 1066, but even then she'd had to browbeat the RAF into conceding that, yes, in this terrible
emergency she might possibly make a combat pilot.

America wouldn't be like that. She knew her own, her native land, much too well. The United States would set up as many training stations as it thought it needed, plus several dozen more for luck. Pilots would flow out of them in a steady stream and then, as things got rolling, in a flood. And every damn one of those pilots would be a man.

Women who already flew? They might let them ferry planes around, as the British did. They might even train some more. That would let them throw men into battle, where men belonged.

What about a woman who'd already flown in combat? What about a woman who had, in fact, flown when things looked worst? What about a woman who'd shot down three Nazi planes?

They wouldn't have any idea what to do with her. A.E. could feel that coming like a rash. When she was flying around the world, she'd seen mudskippers near Singapore—little fish that climbed up on tree roots and mudflats and scooted along with their stiff front fins. That's what she would seem like to the American authorities: something out of its proper element.

They'd win the war without her. She was sure of that. And she was sure as sure could be that they wouldn't want to win the war with her.

"Hey, Earhart!" said Bill Geiger, a kid who'd been with 71 Squadron from the get-go. "You aren't talking much. What do you think of all this?"

"We're going to kick the snot out of Japan. If we get into the fight with the Nazis, we'll kick the snot out of Germany, too. We'll probably need a little while to get going, but we'll do it," she answered.

That met with general approval. It seemed obvious to A.E. Geiger went on, "Won't it be great, flying under the Stars and Stripes?"

She was slower to reply this time. After a beat, she said, "They'll want men with experience—you bet they will. They won't have anybody who's flown in combat except a few old guys who flew biplanes in 1918."

Bill Geiger laughed the heartless laugh of youth. He might not have been born in 1918. "Those fellas won't know much about how we do it now."

This time, she got away with not saying anything. She remembered the RAF sergeant-pilot who'd trained her at Croydon. He'd known what he was doing, all right. The planes changed. What you did with them? Rather less.

When the United States declared war on Japan but not on Germany, A.E. wondered whether Franklin D. Roosevelt hadn't thought Congress would approve fighting Hitler and his gang of thugs. As far as she could see, that was a judgment on Congress, if not on America as a whole.

But it turned out not to matter. Four days after the Japanese bombed Pearl Harbor, Hitler declared war on the USA. Like it or not, America was in the European fight up to its eyebrows. A.E. wondered what isolationist, America First Charles Lindbergh thought of that. As far as she could tell from the London papers and the BBC, he was keeping very quiet. After he'd spent so long making a pro-German jerk of himself, that had to be the smartest thing he could do.

A COUPLE OF DAYS LATER, she ran across a back-page story in the *Times* of London. EAGLE LOST IN TRAINING ACCIDENT, the headline said. A Spitfire flown by an American pilot officer called John G. Magee had collided with another plane on a training flight. Both went down, and both pilots perished.

She scratched her head, wondering why the name seemed familiar. She didn't think she knew anyone called John G. Magee, but still ... Then she remembered. He was the poet who'd written "High Flight," the piece the minister read out at Andy Mamedoff's funeral.

The last sentence of the little story read *Pilot Officer Magee was nineteen years of age at the time of his death.* A.E. looked at that for a long time. Of course, lots of nineteen-year-olds were dying in horrible ways around the world right now. Having this one pointed out made her feel it more, though. So did his being an American, and a talented one.

"'Put out my hand and touched the face of God,'" she murmured, remembering the sonnet's final line. God had touched John Magee now, and he wouldn't need any more touches after this.

"What did you say?" asked another Yank in the officers' mess.

She repeated the line, louder this time, and added, "Remember Andy's funeral? They read the poem there. The fellow who wrote it just died in a crash. He was nineteen."

"Ah, hell. That stinks. That really stinks," the other pilot said, and then picked up his teacup again. Not much more than nineteen himself, he was hardened to death. If you were going to fly fighters, you needed to be. Anything that could happen could happen to you. Sooner or later—likely sooner—it would.

A.E. glanced at the story again. The accident had happened on December 11, the day the Nazis officially went to war with the United States. John Magee had done what he could. Others would carry on.

EVERY TIME she flew a Rhubarb mission into France, she thought of Red Tobin. Word had come back through the International Red Cross that he *was* dead. There was even a photo of the grave where the Germans buried him. Like the English, they were polite to the remains of flyers they'd killed.

She was one of the leaders in a finger-four now. More often than not, Bill Geiger flew as her wingman.

"Just don't do anything silly and we'll be fine," she told him. "You watch my back, I'll watch yours."

"Gotcha," he said, nodding in what she hoped was wisdom. Christ, he was young, though. She really could have been his mother.

Winter weather gave the raiders lots of clouds they could duck into if they ran into trouble. Coming out of the clouds where they wanted to was the tricky part. A.E. remembered Andy Mamedoff, too. But all she could do was all she could do. And by now she knew a lot more about navigation than she had when Fred Noonan did it for her on her round-the-world jaunt.

Still, even she was more than a little amazed when her finger-four came out from under the cloud cover right above one of the Nazi air bases near Calais. Several Focke-Wulf 190s stood on or by the runway. Those new German fighters worried her worse than 109s. By the reports, they were more than a match even for the new Spits: fast, maneuverable, and heavily armed, while their air-cooled radial engines could soak up a lot of damage without quitting.

But they were down there, and she and her friends were up here. "Let's give them some," she said over the radio. She shoved the stick forward to bring down her Spitfire's nose. The others dove with her.

They made two or three passes over the field, shooting up planes and huts. Two of the 190s were on fire when they zoomed north again. The rest would certainly need patching up before going into action again.

Everybody came back to North Weald in one piece, which was the way things were supposed to work even if too often they didn't. "Nice job, Bill," she said. "Good to know things can go according to Hoyle every once in a while, isn't it?"

"You better believe it!" Geiger answered. "Good to shoot at things without anybody shooting back, too."

"As a matter of fact," she said, "yes."

She went in to brief Flight Lieutenant Taylor on the raid. "Way to go," he said when she finished. "The fewer of those F-Ws the Nazis can put in the air, the happier I am. They're supposed to be very bad news."

"I was thinking the same thing, sir." Having said what she had to say, A.E. turned to leave.

"Hold on a minute," Taylor told her. He reached behind him and grabbed a manila envelope. "This came through for you. Go ahead—open it."

Open it she did, and pulled out a sheet of paper. Holding the sheet at arm's length—yes, her sight was lengthening, not a bad thing in the air but not a good one without reading glasses—she saw it was a letter on RAF stationery, informing her she had been promoted to flying officer and signed (no doubt much to his disgust) by Sholto Douglas.

As a pilot officer, she wore on each uniform sleeve a skinny, black-bordered stripe of sky blue. A flying officer wore a fatter sky-blue stripe. Her new rank emblems were in the envelope, too.

"Thank you very much, sir!" she exclaimed, but couldn't help adding, "I never expected this would come through."

"You should've got it a long time ago, if anyone wants to know what I think," Taylor said. As a flight lieutenant, he gloried in two stripes like her new ones on each sleeve. "You've done everything anyone could ask of you and more. The other pilots think you're great. If you were a man, you'd outrank me by now."

She shrugged, remembering Air Vice Marshal Leigh-Mallory's unwillingness to take her into the RAF at all, Flight Lieutenant Darley asking her to cook for 609 Squadron ... and that attempted assault in the dark. She also remembered Andy Mamedoff, on getting promoted ahead of her, saying almost the same thing Taylor just had. Poor Andy!

"Sir, things are the way they are, that's all," she said. "They're still a long way from how they ought to be. But I'm here. That pushes them a little closer, anyway."

"That's the right attitude, for sure." Taylor cocked an eyebrow at her. "If you didn't have that kind of attitude, you'd be screaming by now."

"I keep telling myself I'm fighting on the right side," she answered. "We're making things better, not worse like the Nazis. Two steps forward and one step back, but we are. Maybe I'm part of a forward step. I hope so, anyway."

"You've got nothing to worry about on that score. Congratulations again," Taylor said. She was smiling as she went to her cot to sew the new stripes onto her jacket sleeves. The squadron CO actually got it. One of these days, with a little luck, men wouldn't need to get it. They'd take it for granted. The smile faded. She didn't think she'd better hold her breath waiting.

# CHAPTER NINETEEN

BY THE TIME spring started giving way to summer, she'd been in the original Eagle Squadron more than a year and a half. That the RAF now held three squadrons full of Yanks said all the publicity the first few American flyers got had done its job. But she didn't think about publicity much any more. She was just another pilot doing what her superiors ordered and trying to stay alive while she did it.

Then she discovered Hollywood had cranked out an epic called, yes, *Eagle Squadron*. It starred Robert Stack as the hero, Diana Barrymore as his girl, and, to her dismayed amusement, Evelyn Venable as, well, Amelia Earhart. The guys in 71 Squadron ribbed her unmercifully about that. She took the kidding with as big a smile as she could paste on her face at any given moment.

Flyers from all three Eagle Squadrons were encouraged to attend the English opening in London, and had no trouble getting leave. A.E. wondered how many strings had been pulled, and by whom, to bring that off. If anyone knew, he wasn't talking.

She went to the theater with her comrades. They had two rows of seats reserved for the Eagles, and people clapped as the American flyers took their places in them. Plenty of the men seemed to take that as their due, which bemused A.E.

When the house lights dimmed, she didn't know what to expect. What she got was ... the kindest thing she could think of was, it was something that could have been better. Quentin Reynolds's voiceover made her think it would be a documentary, but it wasn't. It was one more grade-B Hollywood adventure flick.

It did have stretches of newsreel and other genuine war footage mixed in. As far as A.E. was concerned, those were the best parts. The rest ...

Robert Stack was untouchable in the air. Diana Barrymore was improbably beautiful and improbably patient. *Improbably stupid, too,* A.E. thought unkindly. A.E. also noted that Evelyn Venable was at least fifteen years younger than she was. The actress always had perfect makeup when she jumped into a Spitfire (except in the newsreel bits, there were no Hurricanes—with planes as with people, beauty counted). And she shot down more Nazis in the movie than A.E. had in almost two years in the RAF.

Some of the men from the Eagle Squadrons started jeering the picture before it was ten minutes old. They weren't quiet about it, or polite. Before too much more time had gone by, they started walking out, sometimes singly, sometimes by twos and threes as one would nudge the guy next to him and they'd both leave.

A.E. stuck it out almost to the end. Nigel Bruce was actually pretty good as a senior British officer. She liked him better than Sholto Douglas or Trafford Leigh-Mallory, that was for damn sure. Finally, though, the hoke got too thick for her to take. As she slipped away in the darkness, only a couple of Yanks still sat in the seats they'd been given.

Most of the men were drinking at the Crackers Club, down the street from the movie house. Due to her unfortunate femininity, the doorman didn't want to let her in at first. He did relent after the other Eagles loudly and profanely vouched for her.

At least half a dozen flyers asked her something like, "How come the gal playing you didn't look more like you?"

"Ask the people who made the movie," she would answer, or, "I don't know," or finally, when she got good and fed up with the question, "It's Greek to me."

It was a late night or an early morning, depending on how you looked at things. Finally, the Americans headed back to their bases, most of them the worse for wear. 71 Squadron had it quiet the next day. That let A.E.'s comrades recover from their binge at leisure.

Before long, she heard the movie producers and other big shots were sore at the Eagles for walking out.

They got no sympathy from her; if they'd made a better picture, they might have kept their audience. But word also quickly got back to North Weald that the Yanks in 121 Squadron and 133 Squadron had had to fly the next day no matter how much booze and how little sleep they'd had.

Things didn't go well for them, either. They were ordered to escort bombers back from an attack on the German airstrips near Abbeville. As it still did every so often, though, the *Luftwaffe* came up to hit the bombers. The Americans claimed three German planes shot down and one probable. But 131 Squadron had three killed and one hurt, while 121 Squadron lost one pilot and had its English CO badly injured.

A.E. wondered whether the Yanks would have done better if they'd got enough sleep and stayed sober. It wouldn't have been the first time many of them flew with a bad case of the morning-afters. All the same, she wished the movie were better. They wouldn't have started drinking so soon then, or drunk so hard. They might not have, anyhow. Water over the dam now.

FROM EARLY AUGUST ON, rumors floated through the RAF that something big was in the works. On the nineteenth, 71 Squadron found out what it was; British and Canadian troops would land at Dieppe, halfway down the Channel from Calais toward Le Havre. They wouldn't stick around, just smash as much as they could and then cross back to England. With luck, they'd learn how strong Hitler's Atlantic defenses really were.

71 Squadron would fly top cover over the raid, to help keep the *Luftwaffe* from tearing into the soldiers on the ground in France and the ships that had brought them and would take them home again. The other two Eagle Squadrons would be there, too, but 71 Squadron would be in it at the start.

They moved down to Gravesend so they wouldn't have to waste fuel flying over England before they got to the Channel. On the morning of the twenty-first, they went to their planes at 0445. The sun had begun to lighten the eastern sky, but wouldn't climb over the horizon for a while yet.

A.E.'s heart thumped in her chest as the Spitfire's Merlin growled to twelve-cylinder life. Two years before, she'd fought the Nazis above London. Now England was bringing the war to territory they held. That was progress, if you liked.

It was also likely to be the biggest scrap she'd flown in since the Battle of Britain wound down. All told, forty-eight Spitfire squadrons and eight more Hurricanes would try to keep the Germans off the men and ships in the raid. That the RAF was throwing in so many planes argued it expected the *Luftwaffe* would, too.

The sun still hadn't come up, but Dieppe was already burning by the time A.E. got there. Five more

RAF Spitfire squadrons flew with the Eagles in the first wave. She'd hoped she'd be only a spectator. US Army Air Force B-17s were supposed to knock out those enemy air bases around Abbeville, keeping German fighters and bombers from getting airborne.

She'd seen enough by now to know that what was supposed to happen too often didn't. Cloud cover over northern France was thick, which made good bombing harder—how could you hit what you couldn't see? And the USA had barely started learning how to fight an air war. It lacked the RAF's bitterly won experience.

So she wasn't surprised when Focke-Wulfs came up after the Spitfires. She'd heard all the reports, but this was the first time she'd met the new fighters in the air. They proved at least as nasty as advertised. Spitfires started falling out of the sky, trailing smoke or spinning hopelessly out of control.

Some F-W 190s went down, too, but, she thought, not so many. She got a good shot at one, and raked it with 20mm rounds. Big chunks of aluminum skin flew from the fuselage and one wing. The 190 tumbled earthward on fire.

But another one was on her tail. She took a couple of hits before she could duck into a cloud and lose him. She swung hard left, zooming through the blinding mist. The German pilot, damn him, guessed with her. He opened up as soon as she came into sight again. Back into the mist she fled.

She flew as tight a loop as she could, trusting her artificial horizon to tell her which end was up when she couldn't do it for herself, and came out almost where she'd gone in. The German wasn't racing toward her, guns already blazing. She'd outfoxed him this time.

She couldn't read was what happening on the ground. In the air, chaos and death reigned. She radioed an urgent warning to a pair of Spitfire pilots who didn't see F-Ws diving on them from behind. One Spit broke left; the other went right. She thought they both got away.

Eyeing her fuel gauge, she realized it was time for her to get away, too. "Returning to base," she reported, and started north across the Channel. When she brought the plane down at Gravesend, the groundcrew men excitedly asked how things were going. "'Ell of a big dustup, from what the flyers're saying," one told her.

"That's about the size of it," she agreed.

They gassed up the Spitfire again. Armorers fed in fresh shells for the 20mms and belts of machine-gun rounds. Mechanics made sure the bullets that holed her fighter hadn't done any serious damage. Satisfied, they declared the Spit ready to fly again.

Only she didn't. All the Eagles from 71 Squadron came back safely, but they didn't go back to the mêlée over Dieppe. The RAF fed fresh units into the fight instead. None of the Yanks complained. "If they don't want me any more today, I won't cry," A.E. said that afternoon. "I am plumb satisfied."

"You can sing that in church!" Bill Geiger

exclaimed. "I'm not gonna cry if I never see another 190 in the air again, either, let me tell you."

"Yeah." She nodded wearily. The Spitfire V was a fine machine, but with their new plane the Germans had got half a step ahead. Somewhere in England, engineers would be sweating over their slide rules, trying to take back the edge.

Royal Navy ships brought back the Dieppe raiders still alive and able to leave France. England and Germany licked their wounds and drew what lessons they could from the little scrap. Stalin was unimpressed. He went right on yelling for a real second front as the *Wehrmacht* stormed east through southern Russia toward the oil fields in the Caucasus.

Two or three weeks after it happened, A.E. learned that Flight Lieutenant—Wing Commander now—Walter Churchill got killed in the air over Sicily. He'd made a good squadron CO. She missed him. What she felt, though, was nothing like the devastation losing Shorty or Red or Andy—or Amy!—had caused her. She wondered if she was getting numb even to death.

# CHAPTER TWENTY

MORE AND MORE AMERICANS WERE IN London every time A.E. went into the battered metropolis. Their accents stood out. So did their crisp new uniforms. The English, especially the civilians, were trying to muddle through as best they could with what they'd had on hand when the war started. By now, the war was three years old for them. What they'd had on hand was getting pretty shabby.

Americans in crisp new USAAF uniforms also started visiting North Weald and, no doubt, the bases where 121 Squadron and 133 Squadron were stationed, too. Sure enough, they were planning to bring the Eagle Squadrons under American control. They were also trying to learn how an air force that actually knew how to fight a real war went about things.

Most of the men were excited about coming home to Uncle Sam. The United States was their country, after all. And American officers made three or four times as much money as their English counterparts.

Again, A.E. found herself less thrilled. In part, that was because she needed the money less than the other fighter jockeys did. And in part it was because she still hadn't talked seriously with one of those spruce young USAAF officers.

They had big plans for the Eagle Squadrons. They aimed to form all three of them into the US Army Air Force's Fourth Fighter Group. The pilots would keep their beloved Spitfires. That made sense, since America still wasn't building fighters anywhere near so good.

If they had big plans for A.E., they kept quiet about them. She didn't need long to get fed up with that. As was her way, she set about finding out what she needed to know. She went up to a visiting USAAF major and said, "Speak with you for a couple of minutes, sir?" She hadn't quite got his name— Carruthers or Carmichael or something like that: long and with a C.

Like so many American smiles, his showed off good teeth. "Of course, uh, Flying Officer," he said. He stumbled a little before using her title instead of calling her Amelia, but he did it. She liked him better for that.

All the same, her question was blunt. "What kind of place will I have in this spiffy new Fourth Fighter Group?"

The smile slipped a little. "Well, the thought is that you've already done all the combat flying and taken all the chances we could expect from anybody, irregardless of whether it's a man or a woman."

"That's your thought. The Army Air Force's thought." A.E. waited till Carruthers/Carmichael managed a nod. Then she said, "Suppose it isn't my thought?"

"I didn't make the policy. You'd have to take that up with the men who did, the men above my rank." He smiled again, with so much charm that A.E. guessed he got laid a lot. "The feeling is that instead of exposing you to more danger, the Army Air Force would send you back to the States, promote you to captain, and put you on tour to boost war-bond sales and help recruit female ferry pilots to bring more men into battle."

"My feeling ... sir ... is that I'd rather keep on doing what I'm doing now. I've been doing it for a while, and I've got pretty good at it."

"You have to understand," Carruthers/Carmichael said, "there is no place in the USAAF for a woman combat pilot. We just don't do that. We have plenty of men. But you could do important work for us that only you are suited for. You'd help your country more that way. You understand, don't you?"

"I think showing my country a woman can fly a fighter plane as well as a man is the most helpful thing I can do right now," she answered. "Women need to see other women doing these things, so they know they can, too, if they want to enough."

"We don't feel that way about it," the major said stiffly.

"I know," A.E. said. "But I'm still under RAF jurisdiction, not yours. If I can't be a fighter pilot for you, I don't want to come under your jurisdiction, either."

Carruthers/Carmichael frowned. "People back home won't be happy to hear you feel that way."

"People back home did everything they could to keep me from coming over here and flying for England to begin with," she answered. "If the customs men who questioned me when I was crossing into Canada two years ago hadn't thought I couldn't be a pilot because I'm a woman, they would have seized my passport, locked me up, and thrown away the key. Now we don't like the Nazis, but we still don't think women can fly fighter planes. They took a while here to realize women can, too, but they finally did."

Frowning, the USAAF major said, "The United States never liked the Nazis."

"Well, maybe not, but it sure went out of its way to keep Americans from fighting them. Three good friends of mine went through the same nonsense at the border as I did, only worse—they were men, so even customs inspectors could figure out that they might know how to fly."

Major Carruthers or Carmichael or whatever his name was turned a dull red. "I'm sure they'll all be proud to serve in the Fourth Fighter Group," he said.

"No. They won't," A.E. replied in a voice empty of ... everything. "They're all dead now."

"Oh," the American said, and then not another word for close to half a minute. At last, he managed, "I'm sorry."

"Yeah. Me, too, every day, for them and for all the other people who used to be here but aren't any more. You don't know anything about that yet, do you, sir?" If she'd called him *you son of a bitch*, she wouldn't have insulted him more than she did with the formal title of respect.

The red he turned this time wasn't so dull. "A little. A friend of mine crashed in training. They pulled him out, but he didn't make it."

She nodded. "That counts. They're just as gone no matter how they go."

"They sure are." Carruthers/Carmichael tried to bring things back to the business at hand. "So will you go home to the United States and help the war effort along? The country needs you." He didn't stick out his forefinger at her the way Uncle Sam did in the recruiting poster, but he might as well have.

"I am helping the war effort—I'm fighting in the war," A.E. said. "I aim to keep on doing it, too."

"I'll have to report your attitude to my superiors."

"Be my guest," she answered cheerfully, which sent him off in some disarray. People were supposed to shake in their boots when you invoked higher authority. Carruthers/Carmichael didn't know how to deal with it when they failed to. A.E. couldn't have cared less. That was his problem, not hers.

THERE WAS a form to fill out if you wanted to request a transfer from the RAF to the USAAF. More and more these days, there was a form to fill out for everything. A.E. neatly folded the form and dropped it into the wastebasket. She waited for the sky to fall.

She knew she wasn't the only American flyer staying in the RAF. That had nothing to do with anything, though. A male pilot who didn't join the USAAF was a checkmark (a tickmark, they'd say here) on yet another form. A female pilot ...

Before the powers that be could decide what to do about her, they had other things to worry about. With two other RAF units, 133 Squadron was supposed to escort B-17s to Morlaix, in Brittany. Something went horribly wrong. Bombers and fighters never rendezvoused. Strong winds and heavy cloud cover meant the Spitfires got badly off course.

And when they ducked under the clouds, flak and F-W 190s set upon them. More than half the escorts were lost, including every single Spit from the Eagle Squadron. Some pilots were killed, others captured after hitting the silk. One managed to get back to England on his last drops of fuel, but a wheels-up landing left his plane a write-off.

133 Squadron was gone, or as near as made no difference. That put a crimp in the plans for turning the Eagles into the Fourth Fighter Group. Officials vowed that the ruined squadron would be reconstituted, which made A.E. think of dehydrated food. In the meantime, nothing happened for a while.

Then A.E. got summoned to RAF headquarters in London. When she arrived and announced herself, the military bureaucrats downstairs sent her up to Air Marshal Douglas's office. Her heart sank as she trudged up the stairs. Sholto Douglas was liable to order her out of the RAF and into the USAAF to be rid of her and to spite her.

Two other officers went into his sanctum while she sat in the antechamber. Neither looked happy when he came out, which did nothing to lift her spirits. Then it was her turn. She walked in and gave him the crispest salute she had in her. "Reporting as ordered, sir."

"Yes, yes." Douglas returned the salute. "Take a chair if you care to." A.E. tried to hide her surprise as she sat. All her previous meetings with the air marshal had been at rigid attention. He eyed her. "So you'd sooner stay in our service than go to your own country's?"

"That's right, sir." She left it there. Least said seemed best.

But he said, "Tell me why, if you please."

Again, politeness alarmed her more than the brusque bark he'd shown before. "Sir," she said slowly, "you didn't like—the RAF didn't like—letting me fly fighters, but you did it. The Army Air Force won't. As far as they're concerned, I'm just good for raising money to help the war effort. I'd rather go on flying."

He glanced down at some papers on his desk, then nodded. "So I've been given to understand. I wanted to hear as much directly from you."

"Yes, sir," she said, and waited.

He shuffled the papers, looking at one in particular through reading glasses that magnified his eyes. He took them off and set them down when he turned his attention back to her. "I can send you to 609 Squadron again. Not many left in it who were there when you last served in it, but no help for that. It's been a damned hard war, pardon me. They're converting from the Spitfire V to the Typhoon. The changeover shouldn't give you much trouble."

"I'd be glad to go there, sir. Thank you!" she said.

Douglas waved that aside. "Here's something for you to remember if you will. We built the Typhoon as an answer to the 190, which has a clear advantage over the Spitfire."

"I've seen as much, sir," A.E. agreed.

"Quite," Douglas said. "Well, it isn't, much as we wish it were. It's very fast, and it carries four 20mm cannon. Air-to-air against one of the Focke-Wulfs, though ... I shouldn't recommend it above 15,000 feet."

"Okay. Thanks. I will try to remember," A.E. said, and then, "Ask you something, sir?"

"Go ahead. I don't promise to answer."

"How come you're not just making me go back to the USAAF? I know I got you plenty mad a couple of years ago."

He nodded. "You did. But since then you've buckled down, done what you were told to do, and kept your mouth shut. Most Yanks can't manage that last, but you might have been born here. It can't always have been easy for you, either—I do recognize that."

How much did he know? How much did he suspect? Even a tenth of what she'd gone through? She wouldn't have bet on it. All the same, he'd come further than she'd dreamt he could. She answered him with a shrug. "You do what you need to do, that's all. Maybe it will be easier for the women who come after me."

"Perhaps, if we win this time, we truly won't have to study war any more. Of course, they said the same thing in 1918, and see how that turned out." Sholto Douglas put his glasses on again. "Your orders are waiting downstairs. May good luck stay with you, Flying Officer."

"Thank you, sir." Out she went. She might have underestimated him when they butted heads in the dark days of 1940. Or he might have underestimated her, and come to realize it over time. Which didn't matter. She'd stay in the RAF, and stay in the air.

# CHAPTER TWENTY-ONE

609 SQUADRON, she discovered from the orders, was at Biggan Hill these days, an airstrip about fifteen miles southeast of central London. When she walked into the Nissen hut that did duty as squadron barracks, David Crooke looked up from his game of bridge and said, "Good Lord, look what the cat dragged in!"

"Hello, David," she said. Good to find at least one of the Battle of Britain veterans still in the squadron, even if they hadn't known each other well. He was a flying officer now, too, she saw. A moment later, she noticed the ribbon for the Distinguished Flying Cross above his left breast pocket. "What did you get the gong for?"

He shrugged an elaborate shrug. "Staying alive, mostly. Surprised they haven't inflicted one on you, too."

That was British underplaying, nothing else but. You earned a DFC; they didn't just hand them out. She asked, "Who's commanding the squadron now?"

"Flight Lieutenant Roland Prosper Beamont just took over," Crooke replied. Seeing the look on her face at the fancy handle, he added, "He goes by 'Bee.' He's a good egg." He pointed back to the far end of the hut, where a door probably led into the slightly roomier and more private quarters a squadron leader could boast. She walked over and knocked on the door.

"Who's that?" came a voice from within.

"Flying Officer Earhart reporting, sir."

The door opened. Beamont might or might not have been half her age. He did seem to wear command easily, though. "Welcome! Do come in. I hear you were daft enough to prefer us to the Yanks."

"I get to keep flying this way, sir."

"Daft," he repeated, but he stood aside to let her past, then closed the door behind them. Waving her to a folding chair, he asked, "Where does your score stand?"

"I have four, sir—two with this squadron in 1940, two since."

"One to go, then. To the more immediate point, what kind of accommodations can we give you? David says you used a tent before, but you transferred out before the weather got too nasty to make that pleasant."

"Yes, sir." She described how she'd arranged things with the Eagles, leaving out the time that pilot tried to molest her.

Beamont idly scratched his chin. "Corner spots are taken here. Do you mind a tent for a little while, so we can give the bloke we oust time to shift his gear?"

"That'd be fine, sir. Thank you. As long as it doesn't start snowing, I can stay in the tent."

"I heard you were a trouper. I see I heard right. Now, what were you flying in 71 Squadron?"

"The Spitfire V."

"Well, we have some. We still fly them now and again," the squadron CO said. "But what we mostly do is go hunting the Focke-Wulf fighter-bombers that hit-and-run across the Channel. You'll know about those, I expect?"

A.E. nodded. "I sure do, sir. I went after a 109 like that one time. He dumped his bomb in the ocean and scooted home to France."

"Jolly good. The 190's a better plane in the role, though. Even with a bomb under its belly, it can give a Spit trouble. That's why we're switching over to the Typhoon. It's faster, and those four 20mms pack a punch like your Joe Louis. If you can fly a Spit, you shouldn't have any trouble with it."

"Whatever you want me to do, I'll do it. That's what I'm here for."

Beamont eyed her. "Good heavens, where would we be if everyone had that attitude? In Berlin by now, I daresay."

The tent they gave her was bigger than the one she'd had when she was with the squadron before. If she found some way to keep the inside halfway warm in winter, she thought she might like it better than a cot in the Nissen hut. It wasn't much privacy, but it was more than she'd have there.

As for the Typhoon ... She saw what Beamont meant right away. That it could do more than a Spitfire was obvious from the moment she first got airborne in one. Just for flying, though, she would have rather stayed in a Spit. It had what struck her as the perfect combination of grace and power. The Typhoon did what it did very well, but did it by brute force.

She soon found she wasn't the only pilot who felt that way. "It's like measuring thoroughbreds against Clydesdales, isn't it?" David Crooke said. "You'd sooner ride the racehorse, but if you've got to haul a load of bricks you'll take the Clydesdale every time. Well, right now we're in the brick-hauling business." She nodded. So did several other flyers at the mess table.

The squadron soon moved from Biggan Hill down to RAF Manston on the Kentish coast, to be closer to the English Channel and to raiders coming from France. WAAFs there were quartered in the Ursuline convent at the village next door. A.E. kept her tent by the men's barracks. No one said a word about it.

While she flew patrols over the ocean and over southern England, she thought about going down to France and shooting up anything that moved. Sure as the devil, the Typhoon would be great at that. Other squadrons were doing it, but not 609, not right this minute. Everybody had a particular role to play. It was like a movie (and, God willing, would turn out better than *Eagle Squadron*).

When she mentioned going down to France to Beamont, he quirked an eyebrow at her. "Funny you should say that. I've been having the fitters dim the lights on the instrument panel and the reflector sight in my cockpit so they don't ruin my night vision. I want to fly down there after dark and give those Nazi buggers a little surprise."

A.E. had all she could do not to clap her hands in glee. "What a wonderful idea! What does the brass think of it?"

He shrugged with studied nonchalance. "If I come back alive, maybe they'll let others try it, too."

Over the next week or two, he shot up several military trains on the Calais-Paris line. Before long, the electricians started modifying the cockpit lights in other planes, too.

The Germans hit back when they could. Thicker cloud cover let more *Luftwaffe* planes sneak across the Channel. They might not bomb very accurately, but they did some damage and reminded England it was in the war. A.E. hardly noticed when 1942 passed into 1943.

Groundcrew men painted yellow bands on the Typhoons' wings. The new planes looked enough like F-W 190s that enthusiastic antiaircraft gunners sometimes fired on them. She had that happen to her once. Some of the things she said when she got back to the field at

Manston made the other pilots look at her as if they'd never seen her before.

"I had no idea you talked that way," one said, still wide-eyed.

"I don't usually," she answered. "But it's bad enough when the Jerries try to kill us. When my own side does, too ..."

WITH THE NEW RECOGNITION SIGNAL, the fools on the ground opened up on their own aircraft less often. A.E. promised herself she'd shoot back if they ever did that to her again. Luckily, she didn't have to find out whether she meant it.

Before long, the sign for Tiffies changed to a white nose and two white-lined black stripes on the bottom of each wing. A.E. didn't see how the new pattern made any great difference, but it was decreed from On High and so had to be done.

She flew her patrols. She had enough experience to understand that most of the time she wouldn't come across anything interesting at all. Long, dreary hours over the North Sea and the English Channel had drilled that knowledge into her. Not spotting anything was all right as long as nothing was there to spot. You had to stay alert, though. Missing something that was there didn't bear thinking about.

And so she didn't miss the little flicker of motion at

the very edge of visibility. She swung her Typhoon southwest and went to see what it was. That it was heading north raised her suspicions. The silhouette looked a lot like that of the plane she flew, but a 190 would. It was why her fighter was marked the way it was.

She maneuvered to keep her plane between the sun and the stranger. Before long, she saw its engine cowling was dark. It had white-edged black crosses on its wings. She reported her position and said "Attacking the target" as she shoved the stick forward and dove.

It was the easiest kill she'd ever made. The F-W pilot had no idea she was in the neighborhood till she fired the 20mms. The big, heavy rounds slammed into the cockpit and fuselage. Trailing black smoke, the 190 tumbled toward the ground. The enemy flyer didn't get out. She would have bet she'd killed or badly wounded him in that first moment.

"Target is destroyed. Returning to base," she said.

"Acknowledged," said the voice in her earphones, and then, "Well done."

She did a victory roll when she flew over the field at RAF Manston. The groundcrew men all congratulated her on the kill after she landed. None of the other pilots said a word, though. She couldn't decide whether she felt more hurt or miffed. She'd thought they liked her, but ...

The silence persisted through boiled beef and soggy potatoes at supper. After the squadron had finished,

David Crooke stepped out for a moment. He came back with a cake on a tray: a rectangle iced in white, with a black A at the top left corner and another one, upside down to it, at the bottom right. A big black spade sign dominated the center.

"For Amelia!" he said loudly. "Our new ace!"

Everybody whooped. She realized they'd been playing the same game as a pitcher's teammates when he was throwing a no-hitter. Till the moment the cake came in, they hadn't let on that they knew a thing. "Speech!" someone bawled, and they all took up the cry.

A.E. got to her feet. She didn't like speaking in public, but the lecture circuit and teaching at Purdue had taught her how. And these were friends after all, sure enough. "Thanks," she said. "You're a pack of loonies, every goddamn one of you, and I'm awful glad you let me stay a part of—this." When she threw her arms wide, she tried to take in not just the mess hall, not just the strip at Manston, but the whole RAF.

Their cheers said she'd done it. She couldn't remember a time when she'd ever been happier.

# CHAPTER TWENTY-TWO

AS 1943 MOVED FORWARD, she began to see the Allies would win the war unless something really went haywire. In Tunisia, the British and Americans were grinding the Africa Korps to pieces. The Nazis surrendered in Stalingrad, and the Red Army surged west. Then it lurched back again—the Germans did still have some punches left. But if they weren't on the ropes yet, they sure were backed into a corner.

She wondered if the USA and England would try to invade France when better weather came in summer. She saw no sign of it, but also didn't know how much that proved. The cross-Channel air war went on as it had since 1941.

The technicians gave her Typhoon the night-flying treatment Bee Beamont had pioneered. She blasted a locomotive to pieces somewhere near Amiens, then zoomed away. Even in the dark, trains made easy targets.

Patrols and daylight raids went on, too. By now, she hardly thought about them. She just did them. She expected to keep on the same way at least till the landing came. Then she supposed she might fly from an airstrip on the Continent. Shooting up Germany the way the RAF had been shooting up France ...

But the future wasn't real. You couldn't take it seriously. It might not be there for you. The present was an eight-plane Rhubarb raid. A.E. was flying as David Crooke's wingman. That he'd asked her to do it pleased her very much. The pilot who usually went with him was having engine trouble on his Typhoon.

Red Tobin's face came up in her mind as vividly as if he stood in front of her, grinning and joking. He didn't, of course. He never would, not any more. She hadn't been there to try to help him. She'd be there now, by God!

"I'll watch your back," she promised Crooke.

He nodded, and said, "I'll watch yours, too. That's why we fly pairs." He didn't know why she stressed the words so much. The past was as much a ghost as the future. But sometimes, as now, it was a restless ghost.

They scooted across the Channel almost low enough for their props to crop wavetops. The Germans had radar, too. The boffins said it wasn't as good as what the RAF used, but it was good enough to treat with respect. They didn't want to stir up a hornets' nest of 190s and 109s.

Like England, France was going from brown and

yellow to green. Spring was coming on, if you had time to notice it. A.E. had noticed, but only by fits and starts. The mission, how her Typhoon was doing mechanically ... those were the things that counted.

Even in war-focused England, other people had time to pay attention to robins and blackbirds. English robins weren't much like the American ones, except for their red breasts. They were much smaller and bouncier. English blackbirds walked and sang like American robins, but they were, well, black. All that probably meant something, but she had no idea what.

And it all blew out of her head when Crooke's voice sounded in her earphones. "See that smoke plume off to the southeast? It's moving—I think that's a train."

A.E.'s head swung to the right. "I see it," she said. "Shall we say hello?"

"Let's," he said gaily, as if they really were calling on friends.

They went in together. She flew a couple of hundred yards to his right and a little behind him, ready to do whatever she could if trouble came. She tried to look every which way at the same time. As when she'd been weaving along behind most of the squadron above embattled London, that was what she was there for.

They closed on the train fast. But the RAF was not the only outfit to come up with new ideas as the war wore along. A flatcar near the tail end of the train had something—two somethings—mounted on it, one facing forward, the other back. Men were dashing to the rear-facing one, the one pointing at the oncoming Typhoons.

"Break, David! Break!" A.E. shouted into her microphone. "It's an—"

The four-barreled antiaircraft gun opened up, spitting flame and death at the RAF planes. She fired back, but something slammed into her right wing root and sent the Typhoon spinning crazily out of control. She tried to get the canopy open, but the ground was rushing up and ...

She thought David Crooke got away. She wasn't sure, but she thought so.

# ABOUT THE AUTHOR

Harry Turtledove is the award-winning author of the Alternate History works *The Man with the Iron Heart*, *The Guns of the South*, and *How Few Remain* (winner of the Sidewise Award for Best Novel); the Hot War books: *Bombs Away*, *Fallout*, and *Armistice*; the War That Came Early novels: *Hitler's War*, *West and East*, *The Big Switch*, *Coup d'etat*, *Two Fronts*, and *Last Orders*; the Worldwar saga: *In the Balance*, *Tilting the Balance*, *Upsetting the Balance*, and *Striking the Balance*; the Colonization books: *Second Contact*, *Down to Earth*, and *Aftershocks*; the Great War epics: *American Front*, *Walk in Hell*, and *Breakthroughs*; the American Empire novels: *Blood and Iron*, *The Center Cannot Hold*, and *Victorious Opposition*; and the Settling Accounts series: *Return Engagement*, *Drive to the East*, *The Grapple*, and *In at the Death*.

As the Master of Alternate History, Harry Turtledove has written some of the greatest "What ifs" of fiction.

Turtledove is married to fellow novelist Laura Frankos. They have three daughters—Alison, Rachel, and Rebecca—and two granddaughters, Cordelia Turtledove Katayanagi and Phoebe Quinn Turtledove Katayanagi.

Printed in Great Britain
by Amazon